S0-AQM-096

GROWING UP DOUGHNUT

Don Shields

authorHOUSE®

AuthorHouse™
1663 Liberty Drive
Bloomington, IN 47403
www.authorhouse.com
Phone: 1-800-839-8640

First published by AuthorHouse   5/5/2010

ISBN: 978-1-4490-9666-3 (sc)
ISBN: 978-1-4490-9668-7 (e)
ISBN: 978-1-4490-9667-0 (hc)

Library of Congress Control Number: 2010905374

Printed in the United States of America
Bloomington, Indiana

This book is printed on acid-free paper.

FOREWORD

I have lived a full, fascinating life, but some of my memories have faded with age. This book, therefore, could be considered autobiographical creative non-fiction. As Joe Friday declared on the old TV show, *Dragnet*, "The names have been changed to protect the innocent." But in many of my stories, the actual names of my cronies were used with their permission. Most of the stories herein are true of someone's life, but not necessarily mine.

The town of Hoopeston, Illinois, really does exist in East Central Illinois, one hundred miles south of Chicago at the intersection of State Routes One and Nine. The town's layout, as described in this book, is as accurate as memory serves. What a wonderful place to grow up! It had, and still has, the most unique nickname for its high school sports teams -- the "Cornjerkers." All the graduates of Hoopeston High School (now Hoopeston Area High School) are very proud that no other school in the nation (college or high school) uses that moniker.

Hoopeston has a long and storied past, but fell upon hard times in the 1980s. At one time, Hoopeston was home to three canning factories that produced various products year round, but especially sweet corn in the late summer and fall; Food Machinery Corporation (FMC), which designed and built harvesting equipment; TRW, a company that made electrical wire; two factories that made electrical components; and it had a thriving uptown. When the interstate highways bypassed Hoopeston and the east-west railroad pulled up its tracks, this once shining jewel of the prairie fell victim to de-industrialization.

Hoopeston is full of wonderful, optimistic people who are working hard to revitalize their little town. They have large hearts, generous spirits, and open their homes to many during the Sweetcorn Festival in the fall. It is my hometown and I love it dearly.

ACKNOWLEDGEMENTS

I am forever indebted to Susie Dayton for her great job editing this book and for her suggestions along the way. She has a special gift, and her ability to capture the essence of what I wanted to say, and say it better, has been a blessing. Susie lived the stories with me; we grew up together in Hoopeston.

My thanks to all the folks who contributed their memories of Hoopeston and reminded me of kinder times, when people trusted a little more and treated each other a little better. I want to thank my brother, Jim, for allowing me to use some of the events of his life and make them my own. And, as Willy Nelson sang, "To all the girls I've loved before," I think of you often and fondly.

To Bill, Bonnie, Butch, Louise, Mel, Dennis, Debbie G., Debbie R., Don, Rick, Mark, Mike, Roger, Susie, and the many other friends whom I did not mention personally in "Growing up Doughnut," I love you all.

The Kankakee Valley Publishing Company gave me permission to use an old photo that the old Chronicle-Herald of Hoopeston had taken in July of 1968 of Mom pouring coffee for Arnold Schuff after she reopened the shop.

Many thanks go out to Moline Manufacturing of Duluth, Minnesota, which now has possession of the original Lincoln Model D Doughnut Machine, which holds a prominent place in my stories. Moline Manufacturing has retooled the old gal and frequently takes her to trade shows around the world, giving folks a taste of the manna on which I was raised. By displaying my parents' names on the machine, Dad and Mom now get to take the vacations they had always dreamed of.

Finally, Thanks Mom and Dad, you did a great job with us and you worked so hard. Rest in Peace.

DEDICATION

This book is dedicated to Dorothy, my wife of thirty-five years. For many years in my youth, I had searched for *the one*. My mom had been right; *the one* was nearby, just waiting for me to find her. Without Dorothy's understanding and allowing me to go jobless for over a year, this project may never have come to fruition. Sweetheart, you have enriched my life beyond words.

City of Hoopeston

(Courtesy of City of Hoopeston, IL)

CHAPTER ONE

"As you ramble on through life, brother,
Whatever be your goal,
Keep your eye upon the doughnut
And not upon the hole."
(Optimist's Creed)

For over thirty-eight years, these simple words were framed and hung upon a two-toned blue wall in a congenial doughnut shop at the center of the small Midwestern town of Hoopeston, Illinois. The verse was set between images of two jesters, the kind you might imagine in the court of King Arthur. The jester on the left, looking sad, held a doughnut with a very large hole; the other, on the right, wore a big smile, because he had a fat glazed doughnut with a very small hole. These two images and the poem between shaped my outlook on life. The missive would lead me to a life of optimism and allow me to see the good in people and events; it also peered over the shoulder of every person who would step foot into the realm of my parents' eatery, called simply, The Do-nut Shop.

Every day, Monday through Friday, a determined gathering of townsfolk surrounded the counter at this small eatery and discussed the happenings, either fictional or real, of what was going on in their little town. Some of the folks lamented the day like the sad jester on the left, while others attacked the day with the same wondrous gaze of the jester on the right. Like the masks of Comedy and Tragedy, these watchers displayed for all to see that it was not what one had, but the *belief* of what one had and wanted that was the driving force for all of the people who entered and debated as they devoured their doughnuts and coffee. Each person was a mystery to the others as they shared hopes, dreams, triumphs, and heartbreaks. Factory workers, ditch diggers, mechanics, lawyers, publishers, policemen, housewives, teachers, truck drivers, young children, teens, the retired, and the newly employed all came together on their travels to and fro' at all times of the day. For a few moments they were able to evade reality while enjoying the fruits of the doughnut machine that sat in the corner near the front window.

As folks entered the handmade door of the establishment, they saw the counter of the restaurant shaped in a big U, like a conference table of a great mythological king of ancient times, who brought learning and wisdom to his people. It invited people to be comfortable. When seated, they all faced inward toward my father, Jim Shields, the King of the realm, as he listened intently to their stories. His garb was simple and not at all regal. On his head he wore the requisite paper crown, which made him look very military and in charge, along with a V-necked, white tee shirt and a pair of khaki trousers held up by a brown belt. The pants rode just below a round belly that gave him a rotund appearance and made him seem, from the side, to have a Hitchcockian profile or one of Santa Claus, depending on the time of day and the angle of the light. Dad was the master of the grill and keeper of order. No one questioned his supremacy. If someone asked his opinion, they were sure to get it, even if what he had to say was not what they wanted to hear. He watched over everyone and made sure that no one got more of his or her share of grief.

In the morning hours, before the grill was fired up for lunch, Dad would often steal silently from behind the counter to the stainless steel doughnut machine in the corner. There he would help his bride, Queen Alta, create the orbs that people from miles around would come to buy. The Do-nut Shop was the most joyous, popular realm in the county.

Mom was the mistress of the dough. As people listened to Dad, and he to them, Mom was the one who made them laugh and entreated them to join in the frivolity. A frail thing, merely five feet tall, Mom kept things hopping with jokes, stories, and sometimes even song. She was always dressed as though she was a nurse, in a white, one piece dress with a hat, hairnet, and white shoes. Her white stockings hid an ACE bandage which concealed from her patrons an always painful ulcer. The injury had occurred when she was a youth out dancing on a Saturday evening. One of the revelers stepped on Mom's ankle with a high heeled shoe, and the wound never healed until she was in her fifties and had skin grafts to cover the hole.

Mom sat at the Lincoln Model D doughnut machine in the corner for two to three hours during the morning rush, greeting customers and making sure every morsel that came out of the machine was iced precisely with either vanilla or chocolate icing. She took great care in making the icing in which she dipped the doughnuts. She would mix the ingredients of powdered sugar and water with either vanilla or Hershey's chocolate to get the exact taste she desired. On special occasions, she added green for St. Patrick's Day, or orange at Halloween, or red and green at Christmas. Each doughnut rested in the goo until she decided it had had enough and was perfect. She would then grasp the pastry delicately between her thumb, forefinger, and middle finger, give it a twist and lift it out with a quick wrist flip and place it onto a wire rack to cool so the frosting would gel to the proper consistency and drip down onto the sides, the excess running into a tray below. The embrace between dough and flavoring enhanced the fruits of her labor with just the right combination to make them melt in the mouth of the consumer. Mom treated each customer to her warm, perfect, trademark smile.

Behind the hubbub of the restaurant in the backroom and outside its walls, was the real world. Our family of four lived in a small apartment built inside a large storeroom. There, my brother and I lived alongside the King and his Queen. It was there we learned togetherness, respect, and love for others. The apartment was not fancy. We shared the kitchen with the restaurant, so our meals were often taken within earshot of customers at the counter. My brother, Jim, and I had many "relatives" who would often stand up for us, or give us advice. We also took our share of ribbings and were the butt of practical jokes. My brother and I were the Princes of the realm, and were often treated as though we were older than we were. It was this respect that helped us grow up and become the men our parents hoped we'd be.

As children, Jim and I thrived with the advantage of the time and place in which we lived. We didn't know until we were grown that we were accidents during the early 1950's. After their marriage in 1947, our parents were told they would be unable to have children, but there we were, my brother and I, active, boisterous, and often annoying to our parents.

Our small town in east central Illinois was transected by two railroads that ran east/west or north/south. The north/south tracks paralleled the Hubbard Trail, also known as Illinois Route One, or Dixie Highway, the main road between Chicago and Southern Illinois. The interstate highway system had not yet come to the United States and President Dwight Eisenhower would not sign the Federal-Aid Highway Act until August 2, 1956. Drives in the country on single concrete slab roads on a lazy Sunday afternoon were the norm, and we only needed to tell the town telephone operator, Nelly, "Get me Granny's" in response to her, "Number, please," as the dial telephone had not yet intruded into our little town. Hoopeston was a mile north to south, and two miles east to west, and The Do-nut Shop was on First Avenue just west of the Chicago and Eastern Illinois Railroad. From there we had a view like no other of the comings and goings of the people in the community. Gossip flowed like water around the counter, and my brother and I were privy to the stories. We were always admonished by our parents to keep what we heard to ourselves, and we tried as hard as young kids could to not tell the tales to our comrades in the neighborhood.

Because of the popularity of The Do-nut Shop and of our parents, Jim and I were quite well known around Hoopeston. For a kid growing up in a small town of six thousand, this was sometimes good, sometimes not so good. We had to walk a fine line between mischief and malice for fear that tales of our shenanigans would get back to our parents before we did. This fear guided us toward obedience because our father often reminded us, "Whatever trouble you get into out there, your punishment will be twice as bad at home." We decided early on, that we did not like the sound of his belt running through the loops of his pants, nor the words, "Get me the razor strap."

The razor strap was just that, a strap of hide that barbers used to use to sharpen their straight edges. My father had inherited it from his father, so it was a family heirloom, so to speak. The Strap was leather on one side and had a very rough sandpaper-like surface on the other. When the rough surface met the skin of one's bare backside (all corporal punishment involved the removal of pants), it left a distinct impression both physically and emotionally. I learned after the first use of the strap on me that I did not like it. Jim, on the other hand, being older and supposedly wiser, must have been a bit duller than I. Either that, or his butt became hardened to the feel of strap on hide. Somehow that strap disappeared as we got older. I don't know if Dad took to verbal admonishment, or someone spirited it away. Either way, once we reached double digits in age, the strap was nowhere to be found and our family heirloom disappeared.

Jim and I did not have rock star status in the community, but we were well known. All the uptown merchants knew us and greeted us cheerily as if they were saying hello to a family member. We would go uptown, Jim riding his Schwinn, and I on my five dollar junk yard bike, and stop into many of the stores. We were always told by Mom that we should not touch things unless we intended to buy them. The merchants would come into the restaurant before they opened their stores, or they would call and ask for some doughnuts and coffee to be brought to them. When this happened, usually Jim would put the bag of goodies in the basket of his bike and take them the two or three blocks uptown to the customer. I was not allowed to do this until I was twelve and somewhat responsible. The real reason I was allowed to finally do this task for my parents, though, was that Jim got his driver's license and an actual job.

All the while we were growing up, that Lincoln doughnut machine kept going day in and day out. It was a constant as times around us changed. Every day it would crank out a hundred dozen or so, and those doughnuts would lighten the day for those who partook of their doughy goodness, each one a small bit of sunshine and escape from a world that was rapidly undergoing reinvention.

At The Do-nut Shop, every day started with the jesters looking over their just desserts, and ended with the King and Queen closing up shop and sitting alone in the darkness discussing the day's events.

CHAPTER TWO

Doughnuts shaped my life and my physical appearance. Literally. At some point, a friend started calling me "Doughnut," and it caught on just as it had with my brother. In my youth and innocence, "Doughnut," to me, was a reference to the delicious fat pastries my parents served to all who entered The Do-nut Shop. I regarded my new nickname as a term of affection. I did not know I was fat. I was just a boy like all other boys.

Yet, a fat pastry I was in those formative years. The daily breakfasts of two or three doughnuts and milk, and the lunches of hamburgers with doughnut chasers left their mark around my middle. When the Poppin' Fresh Doughboy debuted for Pillsbury in the 1960's, I thought I had a twin brother that Mom had forgotten to tell me about. Pictures of me from the time I was a toddler until about age twelve, show a boy who appeared to be a cross between Poppin' Fresh and the Michelin Tire Man. When I would play in the sandbox in our back yard, and then go in at the end of the day, Mom would make sure I washed between my rolls for fear I would begin sprouting vegetation. But Mom refused to tell me I was fat. She used the terms "big-boned" or "hefty." I wore jeans made for "husky" boys.

My first grade picture from Lincoln Elementary School (which was just two blocks south of our shop/apartment) showed me sitting in the first row. There I was, settled happily and smiling among the "normal" kids, my shoes untied. It was not that I didn't know how to tie them; I just could not bend over to do it. The spaces between my shirt buttons were so far gapped, my stomach seemed to be screaming to get out. Soon after that picture was taken, my mom took to dressing me with white tee shirts under my collared shirts. I thought it was because my dad always wore a white tee shirt, or at least that's how she sold it to me. Many years later, when I found pictures of myself in a box in the back of Mom's closet, I realized I was not "big-boned." I was fat. Luckily, the kids on the block looked past that and allowed me to play with them, or at least they played around me.

Our block was divided into thirds by two alleys which intersected behind my house and formed a "T". These were not the paved alleys of a big city, though. These alleys were dirt, ash, gravel, and full of what we called "clinkers." Most everyone burned coal in their furnaces back in the 50's and 60's and the by-product of the burning was residue that resembled rocks from Mars and were almost like glass, but rough and dark. Clinkers were usually thrown out into the alley to build it up during winter so people could drive their cars down the alley, avoiding the ice and snow, and park in garages that were set near the alley, unattached from the houses. Cars driven over the clinkers would crush them as the winter wore to an end, and the result was a fine dust that then became part of the travel way when the spring thaw came around. Sometimes, large chunks remained imbedded in the dirt of the alley and caused vicious scrapes and cuts when children wrecked their bikes during races up and down the alley. I've certainly had my share of those cuts and have a vast array of scars as testimony to my racing acumen.

Most of the kids had good bikes, even if they were second-hand. My brother had a Schwinn, a red one with cool baskets on either side of the rear tire. He could ride that bike like no one else in town. Jim was almost five years older than I, and he was very athletic. He had not succumbed to the siren song of the doughnut, but was an athlete whom many in the town admired. When he rode his bike, he flew like the wind and you could hear the sound of the baseball cards as they thwacked against the spokes of the back tire creating a sound like a motorcycle as he sped down the sidewalk or street. That is how we used cards back then, as sound effects, not as collectibles. Had Jim not used his Mickey Mantle Rookie card as a sound effects prop, he would be rich beyond his dreams now.

Dad gave me my first bike when I was about five. Until then, I was relegated to riding a tricycle around the block and watching other kids as they rode around the block or up and down the alley. During the day, I rode my trike in front of The Do-nut Shop so Mom could watch me from the window. In the evenings, when traffic was almost nil, she and Dad would sit outside in front of the shop on stools and watch me ride up and down First Avenue. When an occasional car would turn the corner onto First Avenue, either she or Dad would shout, "Car!" and I would immediately turn to the curb to avoid becoming a grease spot on the front bumper of someone's Oldsmobile.

I was so excited when Dad told me he was going to get me a real bike, a big-boy bike. I had visions of a bright red one, like Jim's, complete with side baskets and maybe even some of those colorful stringy things that dangled from the handlebars.

Dad left the shop early one day and strolled down the street toward downtown. I was not permitted to go; he wanted his present to be an event. I was told to wait in my room and he would call me when he returned. The wait for my dad was excruciating. We had no TV at the time, and the only radio station was out of Chicago, about 100 miles to the north. I had very little interest in music at that point in my life, and baseball on the radio did not appeal to me, either. So, I sat in my room made of concrete blocks at the back of the apartment, and read comic books and tried to keep busy with my Fort Apache action figures. Finally, Dad called to me from the patio, "Don! Get out here. I have something for you." I jumped up from the concrete floor of my room and raced to the back patio through the storeroom in the rear of The Do-Nut Shop.

Mom and Dad stood in front of an object they had covered with a blanket. "Son, since you seem to have become master of the three wheeler, Mom and I thought you should now learn to go on two wheels." He stepped back and snapped the blanket off of . . . the most beautiful bike I had ever seen! It was gray and had gray painted tires. The frame was slightly bent and the handle bars were crooked, the basket on the front askew. Dad had gotten the bike from Ruby's Junkyard down the street and had straightened it as much as he could and painted it himself. Others might have considered it about the ugliest thing they had ever seen, but not me! It was mine and my dad had bought it for me.

Grinning ear to ear, I walked around the bike admiring it and thanking my parents. The more I walked around it the more I thought of riding it, and the more I thought of riding it, the more I thought of taking a spill in the alley amid the clinkers. I had seen my friends become bloody messes and suddenly I became a bit wary of this bike. While I had dreamed of the day when I could ride a real bike, it now appeared in my mind as something dangerous and complicated. It did not have a third wheel! There was no way to test my mettle or my balance. Mom clasped her hands to her chest, and with tears in her eyes, spouted, "Let's see you ride it!" Now I was on the spot, and I began to sweat and stutter. My hands were shaking and my palms were wet. How do I get on, from the right side or the left? Do I grasp both ends of the handle bars, or just one? How do I start and stop? All of these thoughts raced through my mind in the fraction of a second it took my dad to lift me up and set me onto the bike. My feet barely touched the pedals, and I had to lean slightly forward to grab the handle bars. The non-padded seat did not fit me right, and caused a rather uneasy ache in my sitting place.

Our patio was at the end of the intersection of the two alleys with a slight downward slope in our driveway, which ended in loose gravel before taking a hard right into clinker alley. Immediately after the gravel, a large hedge that defined the Kietzman's backyard rose to a height of about eight feet. Off to the right of the driveway, was an empty lot that belonged to Mitch's Hatchery next to our shop, and down from that, a large tool shed that housed farm implements for the local John Deere dealer. Reed and Hulse Implements stored many tractors and combines and parts there, and the shed was often my playground. Dad gave me the "Peddle forward to go, and push back to stop" speech, then gave me a good shove! I vividly remember rolling down the slope at break-neck speed with my arms struggling to steer as everything seemed to fly past me: Dad's Packard, the propane tank, the burn barrel, the tree at the end of our property -- then I was off into the alley. I bumped, I thumped, and jumped over things as the bike flew over the gravel at the end of the driveway, careened down the alley, and headed toward the John Deere tool shed. I looked up just long enough to see the large, gray sides of the metal shed coming toward me. Was the shed moving? That's when Dad yelled, "Brake!"

"How do I stop?!" I screamed in near panic.

"Push back on the pedals!"

I did, but there was no stopping my run-away bike. I hit that building like a cartoon character hitting a brick wall. Even though I held tightly to the handlebars, I was launched over them and crashed upside down, my back against the cold metal of the shed. To this day, I remember it in slow motion from a spectator's point of view. I watched from the sidelines as little Donnie Doughnut slid slowly out of the frame, landing in a heap at the foot of the metal shed. I glanced back at Mom. "Are you okay?" Mom did not run to my aid, neither did my dad or Jim.

"Yes, I'm fine," I reported from my upside down position. I really wasn't okay. I was embarrassed and I think I had wet myself.

"Good. You have fun, son," my dad hollered as he turned toward the house with a slight grin. Mom covered her mouth so I wouldn't see her chuckle as she went back inside with Dad. Jim, on the other hand, fell over and laughed uncontrollably at the sight of his stupid little brother still crumpled against the shed. I closed my eyes and waited for the world to end. When it did not, I opened them to see my neighbor, Bonnie, staring at me upside down.

"You're supposed to push backwards on the pedals," Bonnie said. "You okay?" Her tone told me she was glad I was not hurt. Bonnie was five years old, the age same as I. She was practically my sister. Her family lived in a gray, two story frame house that backed up to the shed. She had a round little face that was curtained by brown curls. Her big blue eyes sparkled, and she always had a smile. Bonnie was not the Tom-boy type, but rather a petite little lady who often wore dresses and bows. Her shoes were always polished, and she was very proper. She always reminded me of Margaret in the Dennis the Menace comic strip, but kinder and not as much of a pain.

"Yeah, I'm okay," I replied. "How's the bike?" I looked down at the bike, then back at Bonnie. All at once we both broke into hysterics at the sight of me hitting the shed and sliding down it.

Bonnie's sixth birthday party was responsible for my learning to write with my right hand, and do everything else with my left. Bonnie had invited the entire block and some other friends to her party. The usual fare was served: cake, ice cream, and root beer. After we played Pin the Tail on the Donkey, Drop the Pin in the Bottle, and Musical Chairs, we all went outside to play Tag. When it was my turn to be "it" all the kids scattered to the far reaches of the yard, leaving me, the little fat boy, in the middle. As I began to chase Bonnie, she went through the gate and down the sidewalk, with me huffing and puffing behind. As I followed her around the corner, I tripped on a crack in the sidewalk, went head over heels, and ended up smashing my left arm on the concrete. My arm was broken. When I went to school at the end of summer, my teacher used it as an opportunity to help me learn to write right-handed. It worked.

Having recovered somewhat from the bike crash, yet still profoundly embarrassed, I picked up my wrecked bicycle, steadied the front wheel between my legs, straightened the handlebars, and started walking back up the alley. I suddenly realized that Dad had gotten this particular bike for a reason. He and Mom knew I would probably wreck it a few times, so why waste money on a good bike until I had mastered the basics? Parents are amazing.

"Where are you going?" Bonnie's expression was full of concern. Just a few minutes earlier, I had wanted to just lie at the base of the shed in a crumpled heap. Other kids on the block had heard the commotion by then, and came running to see what calamity had occurred. The girls tittered with their hands over their mouths; the boys guffawed without mercy. It was Bonnie who reached down and rolled me over. "Everyone falls the first time," she had said calmly. "You just have to get back on the bike, and next time, press backwards quicker." Ah, Bonnie Kinder, I thought. There is no one kinder than she.

I shook off my sentimental thoughts and turned my sights to more adventure. "That was fun!" I'm going to try again." Bonnie shook her head and giggled as she returned to her yard, knowing full well that she would probably hear another thump again before the end of the day. To my amazement, and hers, it did not happen, at least not that day.

CHAPTER THREE

At age five, I had gotten my first taste of freedom. I rode my beloved bike around the block until I wore a path in the sidewalk. I must have circled that block a million times, and I knew every brick and every crack there was. Soon, Mom let me venture a bit further, to Joe's, my best friend through third grade.

Joe Broward was a great guy. He was my age, and we shared the same interests. Mostly, we liked to play baseball and army and cowboys and Indians, anything that would let us run around with toy guns or throw things at each other. The Browards had moved to Hoopeston from Chicago when Joe was very young, and once we discovered each other, we were bosom buddies.

Joe had a speech impediment when we were growing up. He could not pronounce his "R's" when they were at the beginning of a word. So, Roy Rogers came out "Yoy Yogers." I never really noticed it until Jim pointed it out to me one day. When I asked Joe about it, he said, "I do?" Then we worked on it to be sure he could say his "R's" right. When I corrected him, he would nod, and then slowly repeat the word so the Y became an R. Until then, we had a lot of bike yaces and yolled around a great deal.

Joe's dad was an engineer on the CE&I Railroad which ran north and south through Hoopeston. The Chicago and Eastern Illinois ran a passenger train from Memphis to Chicago and back. When Mr. Broward's train passed through town, he would blow the whistle extra long, so Joe's mom would know it was him. Since we lived only about a block from the station, everyone on the block knew when Joe's dad was passing through. After Joe and I got real good on our bikes, our mothers would let us ride down to the station and wave as his dad rolled through town.

The Broward house had a large front porch that wrapped around the main part of the structure. We often played under the porch, using it as a cave or a hideout. Joe's parents often fed me and I held the status of "son" in their household, and his parents were my "mom" and "dad." Joe's sisters treated us with equal disdain, and it seemed like we would be joined at the hip forever. I was heartbroken when the Broward family moved back to Chicago in 1962 so his dad could take a position in the train yard.

The trains were good for Hoopeston and for The Do-nut Shop. Trains on the Nickel Plate, which ran east and west through town, carried the goods that the factories of the city needed. The Chicago and Eastern Illinois Railroad's passengers often de-boarded in the middle of the city to rest and get a bite to eat and drink. Many walked the single block to The Do-nut Shop for coffee and a doughnut before they resumed their travels.

One such passenger stopped by on his way from Memphis to Chicago. The train's layover in Hoopeston was about an hour and the conductors sent this traveler towards our shop to rest and grab a bite before continuing the last two hour leg from Hoopeston to Chicago.

As he strode into the shop, the folks at the counter paid him little attention. Mom went immediately to him and offered her usual greeting, "Good morning. Welcome to our shop. We just finished a fresh batch of doughnuts and Jim is getting the grill hot for lunch. What can I get for you?" The traveler was a fairly non-descript man of average height; the glasses on the end of his nose were lightly tinted. He had to squint to see the menu, which was posted on the wall just above eye level.

"I'll have two chocolate doughnuts and a cup of coffee," he said with a gravelly voice that sounded as if it had been dragged through our alley.

"Anything else?"

"Nope, think that will do it."

"What's your name, mister?" Mom always liked to know her patrons on a first name basis. "I'm Alta."

"George, George Halas." Everyone in the place stopped in mid-sentence and turned to look at the man they all knew as the owner of the Chicago Bears. Mr. Halas smiled politely and picked up the copy of the Chicago Tribune lying on the counter. Mr. Halas wore a tan fedora with a brown hat band, a brown suit, and highly shined shoes. The hat was cocked back on his head to reveal a gray widow's peak and a fairly high forehead. His glasses were perched at the end of his nose, not up close to his eyes like I had seen in newspaper pictures of him. He was a fairly stocky man, about sixty, but I could tell he had been athletic at one time by the way he sat straight with his shoulders squared. He sipped his coffee, leaving the spoon in the cup after stirring some sugar into it. "Papa Bear," as he was known, read the Trib sports page as if it was as dear as the Bible, taking in every word on every page.

Folks around the counter pretty much left him to himself. Celebrity did not often come to Hoopeston, and The Do-nut Shop patrons did not know how to approach him. No one pulled out a camera; no one asked for his autograph. They all just let him be to drink his coffee. Except for me. Mom had come into the kitchen to tell us George Halas was at the counter, but would not let me out the door to get near him. I craned my neck to see if I could get a peek from around the door that separated the kitchen from the restaurant.

"Mr. Halas, how's the team going to be this year?" I dribbled down my chin with excitement as I shouted from the kitchen. Jim pulled me back and gave me his fiercest "I'm going to kick your butt" look. A five-year-old knows practically nothing about football, and I was just asking a question that I had heard the customers ask each other. I never expected an answer, really.

"We'd best be better than we were last year, that's for sure." Mr. Halas responded from his seat at the counter. Without realizing it, he now had the ear of the entire place. "Going 5-7 like we did just isn't going to hack it. We need a change, need to get more aggressive on defense and run the ball better on offense." He was starting to get riled up, his face was turning red and the famous vein on the left side of his head was beginning to bulge. Pounding the counter, Halas added, "We don't work hard enough, that's our problem. I need to talk with Driscoll and tell him to get these guys meaner, hungrier. We need to be monsters to play this game. If we don't win the title this year…" he trailed off as he realized his fellow diners were listening and taking it all in. He calmed down and went back to reading his paper.

I wandered in sheepishly from the kitchen and looked at him over the top of the counter. He could just barely see my eyeballs and my flat top. Mom sauntered in and refilled his coffee. "You don't like losing, do you? Sounds to me like you don't think that guy running the team is doing a good job." Mom knew nothing about football.

"The guy running the team? You mean me or Paddy Driscoll?" Halas shot her a look as if he was a judge at an inquisition.

Mom never skipped a beat, and put it all back on him. "The guy who calls the plays, who runs the team," Mom said brightly.

"That would be Driscoll. He's the coach; I just own it."

"If you are not happy with him, do it yourself, if you think you can do better." Mom always had a way with straight talk. She did it in such a way that others were not offended at all. Her voice was calm, smooth, and soft, and her demeanor was always pleasant. But, then again, how many people would argue with a woman who had a pot of hot coffee in her hand? Halas looked at her, startled. One could see that the idea had crossed his mind, but he had not seriously considered it. He and Paddy Driscoll were old friends. They had built the team for many years, but now the wheels were turning. The Bears' performance had steadily declined since taking a sound thumping in the 1956 championship. They had lost to the New York Giants 47-7 in that game, followed by a dismal 1957 season, finishing a deep fifth in the NFL West. Some experts said the outcomes might have been different if Halas had not found himself on the sidelines, always second guessing Driscoll's strategies. Mom's words settled deep into Halas's craw and he set his jaw as he pondered the possibilities.

"Alta, I do think I could do better. I have in the past." And he had. He had stepped down to become president of the ball club as well as its owner. Mom did not know any of this and really didn't care; she just saw someone who did not like the way things were, so she called him to take control of the situation. Her words made Halas realize that he still had some coaching days left in him, despite the fact that he was almost sixty-three.

Mr. Halas finished his doughnuts and coffee and got up to leave, tossing a five dollar bill on the counter. "The coffee and doughnuts are only twenty-five cents," Mom said sweetly. "I'll get you some change."

"I know," said Mr. Halas, "But the advice is worth more." He opened the door and left the shop, strolling back to the train like a man on a mission. The other patrons looked at Mom with their mouths gaping. She had just talked to the owner of the Chicago Bears as though he was a local guy who had come for his daily coffee and doughnuts. Mom took up the fiver, went to the cash register, and rang up the twenty-five cent tab, put the bill in the drawer, and then pulled out four dollars and seventy-five cents and dropped it in the jar she kept on the shelf for tips.

The customers found a new respect for Alta Shields. She had, in effect, told the owner of the Chicago Bears to get off his butt and do something about his team. They were anxious to see if he would follow her advice. Most doubted he would, though he did have a long ride on the train to think it over.

Two days later, the Chicago Tribune sports editor reported the demotion of Paddy Driscoll. Halas would return to the field as the Bears' coach that year and take control as Mom had suggested. Paddy Driscoll would be an assistant.

We never missed a game after that day. Dad went out and bought our first television, a nineteen inch black and white console, which was hooked up to a spiney-looking antenna that sat atop a fifty foot tower outside our home at the back of The Do-nut Shop. The antenna was controlled by a rotor, which had to be turned and tuned to receive each station's signal every time we turned to a different channel. We could get Chicago stations on clear, windless days, but the picture was fuzzy, and we often saw only about half the shows before the picture left us. Oh, but when the picture came in, we were in heaven. We spent every Sunday afternoon during football season watching the Bears play on our new TV.

At the end of the 1958 season, a package arrived for Mom from George Halas. Inside were two Chicago Bears jerseys and a thank you note. Jim got one jersey; the other was mine. No other kid in our town had an official football jersey, so we felt pretty special. I wore mine to bed every night; Jim wore his to school. When Jim related the story to others, no one believed him. How could his mom have influenced George Halas to take over coaching the Bears? Jim could not explain it, but the jersey said it all. By 1963, the Bears had indeed turned meaner and hungrier, and won the NFL title game that year.

The Chicago Bears and the Cubs were our family teams. Dad also followed the White Sox, because their games were broadcast on the radio when Dad came home from fishing in the evenings. The Sox played at Chicago's Comiskey Park, which was located at Shields Avenue and 35th Street. Dad felt compelled to maintain allegiance to the Sox for that reason.

Cable TV came to Hoopeston in the mid 1960's; we now had twelve channels! We could find out what was going on in Champaign, Lafayette, Vincennes, Chicago, and even New York. That was when my brother and I became serious Cubs fans. Their games were broadcast from WGN-TV out of Chicago.

I was glued to the TV in the early mornings when Captain Kangaroo came on. At noon, it was Bozo's Circus and the Grand Prize Game. The Grand Prize Game involved kids standing behind a line and dropping ping pong balls into metal buckets. With each bucket, the prizes got better, eventually culminating in something like a new bike for the lucky winner. I knew, if given the chance, I could drop the little balls into the pails and go all the way for a new bicycle. Parents applied to get their kids on that show years in advance, so I never did realize that dream. I loved to watch movies, cartoons, and serial westerns. I was addicted to the box, as many kids were. But Mom was wise and did not let me or my brother spend hours in front of it, and she did not use it as a babysitting tool. We were required to go outside and play all day during the summer. And during school Jim and I had to do homework at the kitchen table before we were allowed to watch TV. Even though I loved that exciting package of fantasy, I never got to the point where it overwhelmed me.

In reality, technology was changing the universe, yet somehow we viewed the rest of the world as more or less like Hoopeston. The simple life we led in those days did not include much beyond our little town. Between the early 1950's and mid 1960's, Hoopeston saw little change. The Do-nut Shop still had the same light blue over dark blue paint, the same horseshoe counter, the same doughnut machine in the corner. Most customers came in at the same time every day, sat in the same place at the counter, and ordered "the usual." When Mom saw Arnold Schuff pull up to the curb, she would have his coffee and two "crippled" doughnuts waiting at his favorite place at the counter before he entered the door. Mom never charged Schuff for the end of the batch; it was just a given that he would take the leavings. Crippled doughnuts had a barely discernible shape, but Schuff liked them best, mainly because they were free. At lunch, Schuff would come in and have a cheeseburger with a thick slice of onion. Dad would have it ready and waiting for him when he hit the door at precisely 12:10, just after the whistle from the factories blew to signal the start of lunch hour.

Schuff was like a doting uncle who spoils you rotten, then sends you back to your parents. Many days, Schuff would set me up on the stool next to him, tell me about how he had gone fishing or hunting, then tell me to ask my Mom questions he knew I should not ask. Then he would sit back and laugh when Mom got mad at me, and turn quickly away when he knew he'd been caught. One time, Schuff told me to swipe doughnuts from another customer when his back was turned. I was to sneak the stolen doughnuts to Schuff, who then hid them. The victim diner scratched his head, wondering what the heck happened to his doughnuts. Did Jim or Alta Shields take them? Were they planning to replace them with fresh, hot pastries from the fryer? Eventually Dad caught me in the act. After getting to the bottom of Schuff's little game, Dad ordered him to pay for the stolen doughnuts and me to my room in the back. I was not to go near Arnold Schuff for a week.

When I was finally allowed to sit next to Arnold again, he cajoled me to beg my dad for a cheeseburger. Dad gave it to me since it was lunch time. After I ate that one, Schuff said with a grin, "Ask him for another." I did, and Dad made it grudgingly. When I asked for a third, Dad shot Schuff a piercing look, then turned to me and said, "You want another?"

"Sure, they are good, Dad."

"Well, I am tired of your begging, so you are going to eat as many as I fix." At this point, Mom tried to rescue me and told Dad not to fix me any more sandwiches. Dad, however, was determined to teach me and Arnold Schuff a lesson. He proceeded to fix six more cheeseburgers. "Now," he said, "You are going to eat all of them. And you, Schuff, are going to pay for them for egging him on!" Schuff peeled off two dollars and promptly left the shop. He did not want to see what was about to happen.

Dad turned from the grill, plopped six cheeseburgers in front of me and said, "EAT!" And eat I did. I managed to eat two before pronouncing, "I'm full."

"Finish them!" Whenever Dad growled like that, I knew he meant business. I devoured two more and felt as though I would burst. I was sure my belly button was, by then, an outie.

As I started on the fifth burger, my mom yelled at my dad, "James, if he throws up, you are cleaning it!" By this time, I was crying. I knew that if I did not finish, my naked butt would be on display as I got a whipping. But I couldn't go on. Suddenly my gut turned inside out and I spewed all over the floor. Luckily, lunch time was over and there was no one in the place but us. Dad looked at me with fire in his eyes, "Guess you won't bug me about eating more again, will you?" And he marched off to get the mop. I slid off my stool at the counter, thoroughly and miserably defeated, and went to my room. I never again bothered Dad about bringing me more food, even when Schuff tried again. But I learned a good lesson: My stomach had limits. And I never tested its boundary again. Well, not with burgers, anyway.

Chapter Four

Jim and I were afraid of our parents. We weren't afraid because they abused us; we were afraid of disappointing them. They tried very hard to teach us to treat people right. We learned to live by the Golden Rule. We learned to listen to others and not to pass judgment. Church and religion were not to be discussed with friends and acquaintances. Jim and I went to Sunday School at the Methodist Church down the street from our Granny's house on East Main. After church, we would walk the two blocks to Granny's and have lunch with her and stay until our parents came in the old Packard to take us home. I didn't realize until many years later that Sundays were my parents' "alone time." It was much easier and cheaper than sending us to the Lorraine Theater for a two hour matinee.

Granny was born Lucy Bishop in 1886. She was Dad's mother. Her husband, also James Shields, had died at the end of WWII of a heart attack in 1947 before Jim and I were born. Due to his father's death, Dad was released from the military to help run the family business of grain grinding and feed mixing. Granny was well into her sixties by the time I was old enough to retain memories of her.

Granny spoiled us as much as possible and we loved her dearly. Her old two story house was full of nooks and crannies for little boys to explore and hide in. Best of all, though, Granny had a big yard with lots of mowed green grass and plenty of trees to climb. She did not have a TV, but she loved her console radio. We would often sit with her, listening to the voices that dwelled within the old Motorola. Granny loved As the World Turns. She also introduced us to The Shadow, Fibber McGee and Molly, and many other variety shows of the day.

In front of Granny's house was an old hitching post. It was an iron post in the ground with a ring at the top for tying off the reins of horses when visitors came on horseback or in horse-drawn carriages. The hitching post was a perfect prop when Jim and I played cowboys and Indians. I always got to play the cowboy. Invariably, Jim, who was much stronger than I, would capture me, tie my hands to the ring on hitching post, and leave me there. Only after I screamed my head off would he let me go.

One chilly Sunday afternoon in the fall, Jim and I had listened to The Lone Ranger program on Granny's radio in her sitting room. We decided to go outside to play. I was to be The Lone Ranger and Jim would be Tonto. Jim wondered aloud, "What if Tonto turned against the Ranger and killed him?" What? I knew that would never happen. The Ranger could easily take Tonto with his six guns.

Suddenly Jim grabbed me and snarled, "All right, Ranger, I've had just about enough of being your Kemosabe! No more dressing up for you. You are not going make me look like a fool anymore." He ran to the garage and came back with a long skein of rope, dragged me to the hitching post, and tied me up. He did not tie just my hands as he had in the past. This time he wound the rope around and around from my chest to my ankles. My arms were pinned to my sides. Jim had a wild look in his eyes that I had never seen before. I was starting to get scared, but the Ranger would never let Tonto see his fear and I refused to cry. Maybe Jim was just absorbed in the game. If so, he was putting on an Oscar-winning performance.

The Ranger pleaded, "But, Tonto, you've always been my faithful friend! OWW!! Jim, that's too right!"

"Shut up! There's no one to help you this time, Ranger." Jim disappeared into the back yard and soon returned with an armful of twigs and leaves. He appeared crazed as he piled the combustibles around my rope-bound feet.

"Jim, let me go!! I'm going to tell Granny! She'll make you go cut a switch." A few cars had passed by and the drivers honked and laughed, perhaps remembering their own happy childhood games.

"This time, you won't get away, Ranger." Jim's eyes were squinted; his jaw was set tight and there was spittle in the corners of his mouth. He reached into his pocket and produced a rock, and to my horror, a piece of flint. He knelt at my feet and began to strike the flint against the rock. He was going to burn me at the stake!

In a full blown panic, I screamed at the top of my lungs, "Jim, stop! Granny! Graaannny!!" I wet my pants.

Just in the nick of time, Granny stepped out on the porch. "James, what are you doing to your brother?"

"Making him wet his pants."

"Well, stop it. Your parents are going to be here any minute. Now untie him and clean up that mess." Granny seemed not the least bit concerned that Jim might have actually burned me up.

Jim muttered, "Yes, Granny," and let me go. I ran into the house sobbing hysterically and plastered myself to my grandmother's legs, yelling that Jim had tried to kill me. She did not believe me, but I knew it was true.

"Your brother would not do something like that. He loves you very much. Now, go change your pants before your dad and mom get here." Passing through the sitting room, I stopped and looked out the window. There was Jim, on his knees in front of the hitching post. He was still trying to light the leaves on fire with his flint.

Some months later, in the dead of winter, the attempted murder was a fading memory and Jim had not tried to kill me again. Midwest winters can be brutal. One January in the early 1960's, an ice storm had paralyzed the entire eastern central Illinois region. In Hoopeston, most homes had lost electricity as ice laden tree branches crashed and brought down power lines. Mountains of snow and sub-zero temperatures had closed the schools and forced an end to outside play for more than a week. By Sunday, Jim and I were out of our minds with boredom and pent up energy.

Fortunately, Granny's old house was heated by a big oil-fired furnace that required no electricity. Without the aid of a blower, the heat simply floated up through a grate in the center of the living room floor. To humidify the crackling air, Granny kept a big pan of water on the grate. The rising heat was sufficient to bring the water to a scald and send faint plumes of steam into the room. Granny's house was warm and toasty.

Granny was in her kitchen fixing lunch for Jim and me that Sunday afternoon. Unable to play outdoors, we entertained ourselves by listening to football on the radio. When the game was over, Jim said, "Let's play football!"

"Granny won't like it. We're not allowed to rough house," I reminded him.

"Okay, so we'll play in slow motion and use a pillow for a football. Granny won't hear us." Jim snatched a small pillow off the sofa, and the game was on!

As we played, we were careful to avoid the pan of hot water sitting on the grate, moving agilely around it or jumping over it. Granny had warned us often enough of the danger.

Jim took possession of the pillow ball and tried to go around me for a touchdown over the grate. I stepped sideways to block him and he pushed me with his left arm. I spun around, lost my balance, and plopped down in the pan of scalding water. The pain was immediate! I leapt to my feet, screaming, and Granny came running.

"What happened?" she yelled at Jim.

"He was messing around and fell into the pot, honest."

Granny grabbed me, jerked down my pants and dragged me though the kitchen and out the back door where she plopped me in the snow. My little butt sizzled and blistered as it met the cold. "If you boys are going to visit me, you have to do what I say! I told you to never rough house. See what happens? It is all fun and games until someone gets hurt, isn't it?"

When she brought me back inside, I could barely walk. She led me upstairs to the bedroom, put me belly down on the bed and rubbed vanilla extract on my fanny to get the sting out. I laid there until Mom and Dad came to get us.

I thought my parents would be mad at Granny, but they were mad at Jim and me. Me? What had I done? I was the one with the blistered bottom! I could not even wear pants! I was the one who had to walk with my legs spread apart like I had been on a horse all my life! I could understand why they were mad at Jim; he had pushed me down. But me?

The trip back across town was not pleasant. Jim sat up front with Dad and did not say a word. I had to lie across the backseat with my bare butt in the air and my head on Mom's lap. I prayed they would not stop uptown for anything. With my backside exposed for all to see, I didn't want to encounter anyone, especially customers from the shop. My wish was not to be granted, though, as we had to stop at Weber's Drug Store to get some salve for my burned bum.

As Mom exited the car, a bright light must have come down from the heavens to shine directly on our car, because everyone in town converged on us to jaw with my father. Dad rolled down the window, making it easy for all to spy my vertical smile, shining out loud like Rudolph's nose.

"Jim, what happened? Get a little mad, didja? Catch him stealing doughnut holes? That boy's butt's redder than an apple in June!" And Dad, instead of telling them to mind their own business, told everyone how my big brother had tried to boil me for dinner up at Granny's. Jim relished the story, but never interrupted to embellish it. He knew if he did, his butt would get the razor strap when we got home. At least I was spared the humiliation of any of my friends seeing me.

I was never really sure if Jim had pushed me on purpose or if had I lost my footing. Suffice it to say that I learned to respect my big brother's size and strength after being simmered on Granny's grate.

CHAPTER FIVE

There came a day when Granny could no longer stay alone. She had developed diabetes and lost her eyesight and could not go outside to tend her beautiful garden. She could not get from her bedroom to the bathroom or to her kitchen. Mom and Dad helped as much as they could, but Granny would not come live with us. Our little concrete block apartment would be too cold for her. They took meals to Granny and administered her medications morning, noon, and night. Granny had lived through two World Wars, the Great Depression, and had seen man conquer the skies. But she was to see no more.

Aunt Helen, Dad's sister, lived near 63rd and Halsted in Chicago. Her husband, Joe Adams, and their two sons lived in a three bedroom bungalow and wanted Granny to come live with them. Mom and Dad helped Granny move there and sell her house on East Main. I thought we might move into Granny's place and finally get a real house, but Granny wanted to sell it so the money could be given to Aunt Helen to help with her keep. The house on East Main was sold in 1960, and Granny moved to Chicago. Jim and I would never set foot in that wonderful house again.

Our family drove the one hundred miles to Chicago once a month to visit Granny, but it was not the same. We would go up early in the morning in our 1953 Chevy Impala and spend the day with her, take her for a walk, have some lunch, then usually return to Hoopeston the same evening.

Dad and Mom were always stressed about the drive. Jim and I would ride in the back, our parents in the front. This was before cars had air conditioning so summer trips were hot. And, of course, Jim and I always got on one another's nerves. We had no DVD or CD to entertain us; we only had the wind, the scenery, and each other. The AM radio was tuned to what ever Dad wanted to hear. Jim and I played the license plate game, find the numbers game, the spell out a state game, and the ever popular, how long can we aggravate our parents before they explode game. The last game was our favorite, but it usually had unpleasant consequences when we got home.

The Do-Nut Shop remained the same; the machine kept cranking out doughnuts, and Mom kept icing them. The people in the shop never seemed to age, but Jim and I got bigger. Schuff couldn't get me to steal doughnuts anymore, and Clyde McElhaney quit trying to get me to refill his cup, even though refills were free. The folks there were our family, and we often got to regale them with stories of our day after we returned from school, and before we were banished to the apartment.

Jim and I attended Lincoln Elementary School just two blocks south on First Avenue. It was a grueling two block walk, uphill both ways, especially in winter. We had to pass the canning factory and its warehouse. During the time we were in grade school, we saw about a block of houses torn down. I thought that they were going to build an entire new plant, but it turned out even better. The Joan of Arc Canning Company turned that entire block into a parking lot for semi-trailer trucks. What a great place for a kid to have to walk by on his way to and from school. I was constantly amazed at the ability of the semi-truck drivers to maneuver those big rigs around and turn them into tight places while driving in reverse. I decided that I was going to be a truck driver. But first, I had to get over my fear of school.

The very first day of kindergarten was a real heart stopper. I don't think parents remember how scary it was for them. I was unsure of how to act and what to expect. Mom took me to school that day shortly after eight o'clock, walked me to the basement, and introduced me to Mrs. Whitehouse, my kindergarten teacher. She was a nice lady with black hair and horned rim glasses. I clenched Mom's hand as she tried to exit. "Mrs. Shields, you just leave Don with me; he will be fine. You don't need to stay." I immediately wondered how she knew my name. Was this some kind of plot? Was Mom leaving me for another family?

"Are you sure? He has never been gone long from home, except to see his Granny. She just moved to Chicago. He spent many days with her..." Mom started to explain.

"He'll be fine. Go on back to the shop." As Mom turned to leave, I suddenly realized that she intended to abandon me among all these strangers. I knew none of the kids who surrounded me. Some of them were teary with quivering lips; others were bleating like sheep and had rivers flowing from their eyes. One girl was rocking back and forth in a chair in the corner and a boy was sitting near a pile of blocks, yelling and pounding the blocks together. And I was going to be fine? What ever gave this woman the idea that I was going to be fine?

Mom hugged me and then disappeared through the door and up the stairs. I watched as her feet walked briskly by the window and she did not even hesitate to look back. She may have been crying, but I could not be sure because it was raining out. The pit of my stomach began to rise up, and I felt my sides begin to ache. I did not want to throw up all over floor, but I couldn't help it. I started to spew. Mrs. Whitehouse rushed me to the restroom and held my hand as I threw up the three doughnuts and milk I had devoured for breakfast. As I finally stopped puking and crying, she went to get me a cloth. I saw my opening and I took it! I sprinted out the back door, ran along side of the school and found First Avenue at the corner. My feet never touched the ground as I flew past the houses and the factory with its smell of freshly canned sweet corn, and found my way home to The Do-nut Shop. Knowing I would probably be in trouble, I went in the back door by the alley. As I did, Mom was coming in the front door.

"How did it go?" Dad asked as he delivered a cup of coffee to Art Barker at the counter. Dad's back was to me, and there was no way he could see me as I peered from behind the door.

"Fine," Mom replied. "He squirmed a little, but I think he'll settle in." Just then, the phone rang, and I knew I was busted. Art had spied me hiding behind the kitchen door and began to chuckle.

Dad answered the phone, "Oh, hello, Mr. Keller. Yes, this is Don's dad. He what? Do you know where he is? He was seen running toward home? He isn't here." About that time, Art waggled his finger in my direction. "Wait, here he is; he just came in the back door. I'll bring him back."

I stepped from behind the kitchen door as Dad hung up the phone ever so slowly. The back of his neck was red, and Mom had that "Oh, shit!" look on her face.

My father did not say a word as he spun on his heel and scooped me up like a sack of flour. We flew out the front door, which he opened with my head. It was quite a feat as my dad barely weighed one hundred and fifty pounds, and I was about eighty pounds. He clutched me firmly to the side of his hip until he unceremoniously plopped me in the front seat. We had a great audience as he backed out of the parking space, slammed the transmission into gear, and spun the tires on the Chevy as we raced back down the street. The two block drive went in a flash with not a word being spoken. I could tell by Dad's jaw line that he really did not want to talk, but was on the verge of yelling. He held it back incredibly well, although the bulging vein in his forehead had turned a deep purple.

As we arrived at Lincoln Elementary School, First Avenue was blocked by barricades. The school was separated from the play ground by the street, so the town administrators allowed the school to block off the street between so kids could cross safely to the play area where the swings and ball fields were. The sawhorse barrier did not stop Pop though, as he swerved around it and came to a halt in front the sidewalk leading to the school doors. "Get out!" he commanded. I did not wait for him to tell me a second time, and I pushed open the heavy car door. As my feet hit the wet brick pavement, Dad suddenly appeared next to me. He grabbed my hand and rushed me through the rain, into the school, and down the steps to the kindergarten room. We were met at the door by Mrs. Whitehouse. "Thanks, Jim, I am so sorry for the trouble." Dad looked her in the eye, winked, and told her to stop by the shop to get some doughnuts the next day for the faculty. Then he looked at me and said pointedly, "Behave." I had no problem with kindergarten from that day on.

Mornings were fantastic for a kid in kindergarten. We got there around eight-thirty, played, colored, played some more, came back inside for milk and a snack, learned some words, then took a nap. When we woke, we went outside again to play, then got ready to go home by noon. What was there not to like?

I had been dubbed, "The Runner" by my classmates, which was totally ironic since I could not run worth a damn. At recess, I could barely put one foot in front of the other without oxygen, and when moving as fast as I could, I must have looked like the tortoise in the fable to the other kids. But, I could talk and I could spin a yarn, so I had more than a few friends.

First grade had been pretty much wasted for me. We did not have milk and cookies in first grade, and the lack of a nap wreaked havoc with my system. I would fall asleep at my desk while doing my work, and the teacher would skulk up behind me, grab me by the nape of the neck, and then knock my head on the wooden desk. This was supposed to make me not fall asleep? Well, it worked. By the end of first grade, I could read better than most kids, but I still had trouble with the exercise thing.

Sometime during the middle of second grade, my teacher, Mrs. Stark, told Mom and Dad that I should have my eyes tested. I was having trouble seeing the blackboard. Could it be that my head had been bashed so much that my eyes were out of whack? Doc Baldwin checked me out and found that I did have astigmatism, and fitted me with my first pair of bottle end glasses. From then on, I always wore glasses, and to some people it seemed as though I peered at them through fish bowls. The frames were rather stylish with horned rims, and I kept this look through high school. Glasses did not stop me from talking and making the other kids laugh.

It was in second grade that Mrs. Stark struck a chord in my heart. She thought I could be an entertainer. She allowed me lots of leeway when it came to talking, and I flourished in her class.

Mrs. Stark's classroom was huge. Not only did it have room for thirty desks, it also had a short wall to cordon off the little space where we hung our coats on hooks. The wall was not very high and Mrs. Stark would watch us as we put away our things. It served many purposes; one was to be a stage for me on Fridays when I performed my puppet shows.

Mrs. Stark had a fine way of getting work out of me. If I did not get my math done, no puppet show. If I did not get my geography coloring done, no puppet show. I loved performing for the class with my Three Stooges puppets. I would watch the shows that were on Channel 3 after school and then put together a show with my hand shoved up the puppets' behinds. I was very clever with the voices . . . "nyuck, nyuck, nyuck." I had Curly down pat, and all I needed was a pencil for Moe to smack someone with. Larry was more difficult to imitate, and I only had two hands, so Curly and Mo were my "go to" stooges.

The name "Doughnut" began to make its way into my classmates' vocabulary. They had stopped calling me The Runner about mid-year in favor of my new name. Mrs. Stark thought, as I did, that "Doughnut" was a take on my folks' shop, so she let them continue. From then on, I was Donnie Doughnut, or just Doughnut. Then my classmate, Billy Gholson, told Mrs. Stark the kids were making fun of my rotund figure, not honoring my parents' shop. She admonished the class about name calling, but "Doughnut" stuck to me for rest of my school days in Hoopeston. Gholson became my best friend, forever and ever, Amen.

Third grade was largely uneventful. I did not get to perform much there because we had a lot of work to do. Third grade seems to be the milestone at which teachers think students are ready for homework. We worked in class, but what we did not get done, we had to take home and finish. I brought a lot of work home, not because I couldn't finish the work at school, but because I wanted to do it at home. Mom loved it when I sat at the kitchen table and did homework. She would be at the sink or cooking at the stove, and she would sing while I studied. Sometimes I would ask her questions just to see if she was paying attention. Her answer was usually, "What do you think? I would tell her and she would ask, "Why is that right?" And I would explain it to her. It was very hard for a third-grader to teach an adult, but Mom was a quick study, and I was patient with her. Years later, I realized she had not been asking me questions so she could learn the answers. Alta Shields was teaching me to think, while quietly allowing me to believe that I, little Donnie Doughnut, was the teacher. I came to know as I grew up and met other families, not all moms are like that. I had been blessed.

Performance came back into my life in the fourth grade. It was there that Mrs. Goodrum inspired me to learn about public speaking. Fourth grade was basically a repeat of the third, but Mrs. Goodrum found ways to keep us moving forward. She would have us memorize poems and stories, then repeat them aloud. Many of the kids did not like it, but I ate it up. I was a natural ham and loved being the center of attention. I told Mrs. Goodrum I was going to memorize Lincoln's Gettysburg Address by Memorial Day. She promised that if I did, she would make sure I would be permitted to recite it at Memorial Day services at Floral Hill Cemetery. I worked the entire second half of the school year memorizing that speech. Whenever I had time, I would ask Mom to listen to me. I even bugged customers at The Do-nut Shop to coach me.

Abraham Lincoln had always enthralled me. His greatness as a president and his sudden death moved me to wonder how things might have been different had he not been assassinated. I discovered that a relative of mine, General James Shields, had once challenged Abe Lincoln to a duel because Mrs. Lincoln had made some derogatory remarks about him. When they went to the field to duel, Mr. Lincoln chose swords as weapons. When he held his sword out toward General Shields, the general discovered that Lincoln could kill him from six feet away. General Shields decided to accept Lincoln's apology and the two became friends. Lincoln went on to become president, and Shields served in the military as the general who defeated Stonewall Jackson.

February of 1962 was one of the most exciting times I remember. Astronaut John Glenn provided that excitement. President Kennedy had made a promise that the United States would put a man on the moon by the end of the 1960s, and with Lt. Colonel Glenn going into orbit, that promise was well on its way to fulfillment. I begged Mom the night before to get me up early and watch the blast off from Cape Canaveral, and true to her word, she woke me up, fixed me breakfast and I sat down in front of the TV at about 5:30 as Walter Cronkite was talking about how the mission was going to work. Glenn would make three complete revolutions of the globe and splash down in the Atlantic Ocean about four and half hours after liftoff. The idea of space flight enthralled me. I had already watched Alan Shepard go up for his suborbital flight, so Glenn's three orbits mesmerized me. I was not to see it live though, as I had to go to school before the 8:45 liftoff.

All day long I thought of little else but John Glenn orbiting the earth and how wonderful that must have felt. It's hard to concentrate on math and English when there were dreams of space travel to be had. When school was dismissed for the day, I raced home to catch the news. I could not get enough of the scene as time and again, I watched Friendship 7 go into the air in what was described by Astronaut Glenn as a "fireball." The world had suddenly become smaller and more mysterious. Nothing now seemed impossible as people began exploring the last frontier.

As spring arrived, the Shields family often took to exploring the countryside on Sundays since Granny had moved Chicago to live with Aunt Helen and Uncle Joe. With the car windows open, the sweet smell of new grass and corn, tomatoes, and asparagus sprouts filled us with expectation. My grumpy brother was weary of hearing the "Gettysburg Address," but he found it in his heart to encourage my dream of reciting President Abraham Lincoln's famous speech on Memorial Day. We often stopped at Floral Hill Cemetery so I could practice my speech on site. I had only one more paragraph to memorize. "And the government of the people, by the people, and for the people . . ."

One late April afternoon, we arrived home to hear the telephone ringing. This was unusual, as we seldom received phone calls. Our hometown friends usually came over if they wanted to talk. "Hello? Yes, this is Jim Shields." Dad's voice dropped to almost a whisper. "Go ahead, Nelly, put her on. Helen?" Aunt Helen rarely called us from Chicago, so we all stood still and looked at each other with alarm. Several seconds passed as my father's face eclipsed and fell. With an unsteady voice, he said into the phone, "All right, I'll call Hamilton's Funeral Home and take care of . . . make arrangements. Yes, I'll let you know. Bye."

Dad turned his face to the wall as he hung up the phone in The Do-nut Shop. After a deep breath and a shudder, he turned back to us. "Boys, your Granny is dead. She passed away in her sleep during her nap just an hour ago." A tear spilled from his eye, then another, and another. Suddenly, heaving sobs of great loss, Dad disappeared through the kitchen door and into our apartment. Mom quickly grabbed us up in her arms and kissed us both, then went to be with Dad. Jim and I were speechless, not knowing what to say or do. We had never dealt with death before, and we had never seen our father cry. Jim and I sat at the counter of The Do-nut Shop. He looked over at me and said with a croaky voice, "Granny is not going to be with us anymore, you know. We won't go to Chicago and see her."

"What happens now?"

"Well, there will be a funeral, then they will bury her in the ground."

"Will she be cold?"

"No." Jim seemed to have an uncanny knowledge of the future. His four, nearly five year advantage on me had given him wisdom I never knew he had. He was pretty calm about it, but I could tell by his reddening eyes that he was going to cry, too.

After a short time, Dad emerged from the apartment composed and dry-eyed. He picked up the phone receiver.

"Number, please?" Nelly inquired.

"Nelly, can you ring Hamilton's? Yes, at the funeral home. We have had a death in the family. My Mom, up at Helen's in Chicago. Thanks."

Nelly was a sweetheart. She knew everything about everybody in Hoopeston. She knew about births, deaths, breakups, who was dating whom, who lied, who cheated, who got caught, who got fired, who moved into town, and who moved out. But she never spilled the beans on anyone. I wonder if Ma Bell ever knew what a fine employee Nellie was. We in Hoopeston knew. And we all loved her.

Dad made the arrangements at Hamilton's Funeral Home. Before the ceremony, the family gathered in the viewing room where Granny lay in her casket. She was my first experience with death and I had never seen a dead body before, so I wasn't sure what to expect. Granny was in her favorite blue dress and her silver hair was perfectly done. Her glasses rested upon her nose ever so slightly and those hands that had rescued me from boiling alive were folded neatly at her waist, clasping each other. I stood there for the longest time because I would swear I could see her breathing. As I reached out and touched her hands, their chill passed through me, and I felt a sudden shiver. I then realized that I would not see her in this world again, and I leaned over and kissed her on the forehead. It was almost as if she told me things would be alright, as suddenly I felt at peace.

Granny's funeral was a simple one. The Methodist minister gave a nice speech. A lovely lady sang, "Amazing Grace," then we rode in our car behind the hearse to Floral Hill Cemetery and stopped at the grave site. There, six men took the casket from the back of the hearse and rested it on a platform above the grave.

Granny's grave was next to her husband, James Russell Shields, for whom my brother had been named. He had moved from Fleming County, Kentucky to Hoopeston where he met Granny. People told me and I had seen in pictures that Dad and Grandpa looked so much alike, they could have been brothers. They each had that round belly, and slumped shoulders, and their facial features were very much alike. As the minister again went over the Twenty-third Psalm, I wondered what Grandpa must have been like. I mused that Granny was much like my own mother, and therefore Grandpa must have been much like Dad.

When the service ended, many residents in the town came to The Do-nut Shop to offer condolences. The ladies of the Methodist Church Auxiliary brought food for thousands, or so it seemed, as the entire counter was lined with a veritable buffet. Family, friends, and patrons came and went throughout the afternoon. Dad introduced Aunt Helen and Uncle Joe, as well as my cousins, Jim and JD, to the people who came that day. Aunt Helen had moved to Chicago from Hoopeston a number of years back, but she remembered the names of many of the folks. Jim and I kept a low profile, and hardly anyone sought us out.

The two jesters overlooked the gathering from their perch on the wall as guests told stories about Granny and Grandpa Shields and how they had started their own business, a feed grinding mill, and became successful. As the stories flowed, the mood changed from somber to reserved gaiety. In the late afternoon, Aunt Helen and Uncle Joe and their boys loaded up their Pontiac and drove home to Chicago. Our family never went to Chicago to visit them. I guess that after Granny was gone, the impetus to go to the big city never was strong enough to fuel Dad's desire to go there. I didn't see anyone from Dad's side of the family for several years.

True to her word, Mrs. Goodrum arranged for me to deliver the Gettysburg Address at Floral Hill a month later on Memorial Day. It was a beautiful day, with the high school band nearby and flowers and flags on almost every grave. As I stepped to the podium to deliver my speech, I looked around and realized I stood within one hundred yards in any direction of my ancestors' graves: Granny and Grandpa Shields, Great Grandpa and Grandma Bishop, Grandma and Grandpa Ervin, and a myriad of cousins, uncles, and aunts. I could feel their presence as I performed for them. ". . . and we here highly resolve that these dead shall not have died in vain . . . shall not perish from the Earth."

As I finished the speech, the crowd applauded politely. A small breeze kicked up and the trees rustled sounding as if they, too, were pleased with those famous lines. Lincoln had said those words almost one hundred years earlier when he had been invited as an afterthought to Gettysburg. His speech lasted just over two minutes as he did not want to take time away from the main speaker of the day, noted orator Edward Everett, who spoke for over two hours.

The calming words of Lincoln's Gettysburg Address helped me through some difficult times and would come to mean more to me in the years ahead.

CHAPTER SIX

Summers in Hoopeston were one long recess. Kids would get up in the morning, have breakfast, and then head out for the day. We would stay out all day and get home before the streetlights came on. Mothers would communicate and let each other know where we were, so there was very little need to check in. If one kid wanted to go to another's for lunch, no problem, one Mom would call the other and let her know. Moms always had a sense of where we were, and if something was wrong. Kids seldom strayed away from the block where they lived, so a mere shout out the back door would usually suffice to call a youngster home. When we were allowed to go off the block, mothers always knew where we were, no cell phones or GPS needed. They had "Momdar" which seemed to work under any circumstance and in any weather. Quite often, when we were around another kid for a long time, we called their mom "Mom." Rarely did we even know the other mother's first name, and heaven forbid we should call them by it, but rather always put a "Mrs." in front of their last name.

Dial telephones were relatively new in our little town, even though they had been around in the big cities for quite a while. But playmates did not call each other often. We all knew how to get together to have fun. We played baseball, football, basketball, ran races, had bike races, climbed trees, and generally had fun without organizations telling us how. Someone always had a baseball game going at John Greer Junior High School or at the Little League Park out by the John Deere Vermilion Works. The older boys played at the Pony League field at McFerren Park. Kids on the north side played at Honeywell School and those on the east side went to Hoopeston High School to play. There was always a game somewhere. All a kid had to do was show up, bring a glove and a bat, and they were in. There were a few girls who played, but for the most part ball games were for males only. It seemed guys could play baseball all day. We brought water, pop, and food, and rested under shade trees between games. If we ran out of water, we went to a house nearby and got water out of someone's garden hose. Nobody minded.

Each group had a leader who took responsibility for getting everyone together. Our organizer was Butch Drollinger. Everyone looked up to Butch because he was the most athletic and was more physically developed than the rest of us. His real name was Harold, but no one called him that. Harold did not seem to fit him, but Butch was perfect. The name was short, to the point. And that is what Butch was . . . to the point. He could hit a ball a mile it seemed, but not as far as my brother, Jim, who was four years older than Butch.

Although I didn't see it, local legend has it that Jim hit the longest homerun in Little League history. The Little League fields were located near a set of gas storage tanks a block away and across a set of railroad tracks. One summer night, in his last year of Little League while playing for one of the sponsored teams called Silver Brothers, Jim came to bat with the score tied in the bottom of the seventh inning. A storm was coming in from the west, and the umpires wanted to get the game over before the lightning came. Jim faced his good friend, Steve Frasier who played for a team sponsored by Wallace Agency. Steve threw a pitch just off the plate trying to get Jim to swing at it, but Jim reached out and connected just as a bolt of lightning raced across the sky. The ball exploded off the wooden bat and traveled in the air the full distance to the tanks and bounced off one halfway up. The ball was estimated to have traveled almost two blocks after taking in the length of the field and distance of the tanks from the tracks. The ball eventually ended up near Main Street, another one hundred feet from where it impacted the tank. I always wanted to do that, but the baseball gods never came together to allow me to do it.

We played games all summer during the day with no adults to bother us. If there was a dispute, we settled it either by tossing the bat and having our hands climb to the end, or by duking it out. Things usually didn't get that far; when tempers flared we took a break. Occasionally, an angry kid would take his bat and ball and go home, ending the session. But by and large, arguments were rare.

Teams could be formed by any number of kids; we did not care if we were playing with five on a side. As long as we had a couple infielders and a couple outfielders, the game was on. We played *pitcher's hands out* or *nail the runner with the ball*. Once a game started, players were added as they came to the fields. Everyone got to play, no matter how bad they were.

Baseball was king during the summer months, especially in the mornings. We were left alone to play our little hearts out. The adults got involved during the evenings when Little League and Pony League games were played. Most of the boys played in one of the leagues, with the kids over thirteen playing in the Pony League at McFerren Park, and the younger kids in Little League.

Afternoons were spent in the big swimming pool at McFerren Park. The pool was the best hangout on those hot, sticky days, and it was usually packed to the rim. The concrete structure was built into an island in the middle of the lagoon. To get to the pool, one had to walk across one of two rickety bridges. Once there, people usually stayed all afternoon. McFerren Park used to offer boat rides on the lagoon in the first half of the twentieth century, but that had all disappeared by the time I came along.

The pool was divided into three sections. There was a baby pool, about two feet deep, separated by a concrete wall from the deeper water. Then there was a middle section that sloped from three feet to six feet deep. The middle section was separated from the really deep end by a rope that had rubber floats on it. The deep end was over ten feet deep at the far end of the pool.

All the kids wanted to go into the deep end, but first they had to pass a test. The test was relatively simple; jump off the three meter board, jump off the ten meter board, swim the distance across the pool and back, and tread water for one minute. Some kids had trouble passing the test, and I was one of them.

Swim tests were conducted at mandatory rest times in front of everyone. The added pressure and embarrassment of not completing the tasks were often the downfall of many kids, myself included. I was afraid of the high dive, because of the pain I imagined I would feel as I hit the water. What if I don't come up? What if I belly flop? Would it hurt my boy parts? Add in the thought of failing in front of my peers, and it took me a while to muster the courage.

I learned that if one is to try something new for the first time, it should be done as privately as possible. So, I picked a cool, cloudy day when few swimmers would be at the pool. It was a perfect. There were only three lifeguards and about ten other swimmers, whom I did not know, in the pool. I asked Mr. Forshier, who managed the pool, if I could do the test and he said yes. At the rest break, which came around every forty-five minutes, Mr. Forshier yelled for me to get ready for my test. I decided to jump off the high board first because it really scared me. Once that was out of the way, the rest would be a cake walk. I climbed to the top of the platform and walked gingerly out onto the plank. This must have been what pirates felt like, I thought. My body was quivering as I looked over the edge.

"Don't think, jump!" Mr. Forshier yelled at me from the side. I covered my eyes and held my nose and stepped off the edge. The feeling of falling almost made my lunch revisit my mouth and seemed to last forever. After I hit the water, I opened my eyes to see the ladder through the watery haze and quickly struggled to the side. Mr. Forshier grabbed me as I surfaced. "Great job! The hard part is done! Now let's go to the low dive." I pulled myself out of the pool and didn't have time to bask in the joy of my accomplished as he whisked me on to my next task. After the thirty-foot drop, the low board was nothing. I actually ran off the edge and into the pool! When I came up, Mr. Forshier yelled, "Tread!" This required some coordination. I had to kick my feet and move my arms in a circular motion to keep my head above water. For me, it was like patting your head and rubbing your belly; there was a degree of difficulty that I had not counted on. One minute is a long time. But I did it! At the end of the minute, Mr. Forshier yelled for me to come over to the side so I could begin the final leg of the test, swimming across the pool and back again. Although I could swim, I was by no means an expert, and I had trouble getting breaths. I pushed off the side and started swimming. The three lifeguards had been my instructors during swim lessons and they knew this would be a struggle for me. They all perched upon their chairs like eagles ready to pounce on prey. Halfway across the pool, I stopped for a breath of air, and one of the guards came out of her chair, poised to jump in and save me. But I stayed the course and resumed swimming. At the other side, I held on for a second, panting heavily, and then pushed off for my return trip. Somehow, on that last leg of the test, I developed a rhythm and actually made it back across the pool without stopping. As I grasped the side, I heard the guards yelling, "Great job! Way to go!" From then on, I was allowed to go into the deep end of the pool. I have always been amazed how that simple act of confronting my fear of the high dive has helped me through the years.

Bike rides were the summer norm as the apron strings became looser. Mom and Dad allowed me ride to the other side of town to go to the library or to my cousins' houses on the north and east sides of town. My parents admonished me to watch out for drivers because they would not watch out for me. My favorite ride was to the library through uptown. I would take the alley between Main and Penn Streets to avoid being a danger on the sidewalk in front of the shops and businesses. I took a quick short cut home that was down hill and gave me plenty of momentum as I whizzed by York's Barbershop and onto Bank Street. I loved the thrill of going fast and developed a bad habit of not looking out for cars. I was soon to learn that Mom and Dad were right. Drivers were not looking out for me.

About mid-July, before I entered fourth grade, Joe Broward came over and asked if I would go up to the library and get a book for him. He was grounded for not doing his chores, but his mom let him come to my house and ask for a book.

"Could you go up to the library and get me that book on the Flying Tigers?"

"Sure. I'll go after I get my chores done. I don't want to end up like you and not be able to go outside! I'll get it about three or so, is that too late?"

"Nah, three's good. I got a feeling I'm going to be locked up for a while. Mom's pretty mad at me and Dad comes home on the train this afternoon. I'll either be in my room until school starts, or I'll have to eat standing up for a while." Joe spoke as though he had received a life sentence.

I got my room cleaned before noon, and then went next door to Mr. Mitchell's hatchery. He had live chickens and a cow, and he paid me a dollar a week to feed them. The feed bucket was always hung next to the door for the calf, who always came up to me and licked me with his big, rough tongue. It was easy to feed the calf, but I didn't like feeding the chickens. They would squawk and peck at me when I took their food tray away to fill it. Sometimes the chickens in the upper pens would kick food and God knows what else down on me. When the chickens were old enough, or Mr. Mitchell could not sell them, they were taken out back and unceremoniously beheaded with an ax, I had heard the phrase, "running around like a chicken with its head cut off," but I didn't think that was possible until I saw it happen. It made me wonder if people beheaded in the French Revolution ran around like chickens with their heads cut off. I couldn't find anything about that at the library.

About three o'clock I remembered I was supposed to get a book for Joe. I took off on my bike, bypassed the uptown as usual, and got to the library. The librarian helped me find the book Joe wanted. I put it in my basket and headed towards home. I made the right turn into the down hill alley and began to pick up speed. The breeze and the shade of the buildings felt good against my face and my mind wandered to the upcoming school year. I don't remember passing York's Barbershop or gliding onto Bank Street. I was just going fast and loving it!! I was jolted back to my senses as my bike hit a car traveling south on Bank. The impact sent me airborne. I vividly remember flying ass over teakettle from the middle of the street to the opposite sidewalk, landing in a heap at the feet of two local doctors who were leaving their office for the day. Dr. Strzembosz and Dr. Fleisser picked me up, carried me into the clinic, and laid me on a table. The next thing I knew, Mom and Dad were standing over me.

"Didn't look both ways, did you? Dad questioned. He had this look on his face which was neither mad nor upset. I certainly did not want to get into anymore trouble than I already was.

"No, sir, I didn't."

"What were you doing riding uptown anyways?"

"Getting a book for Joe from the library."

"Well, you won't be going to the library any time soon. Your arm is broken and your leg is badly bruised."

"How's my bike?"

"Don't worry about that. Worry about the dent you put in Mr. Livingston's car!" Mom stood by and covered her mouth with her apron. I don't know if she was upset because of the wreck, or if she was laughing. They gathered me up and took me the two blocks home. I was put onto the couch and told to stay there unless I had to go to the bathroom. Joe came over after dinner to see me. "You okay?" he asked sheepishly as he came into the room.

"I'm fine. I got your book. Mom put it on the table in the kitchen." He made his way to the kitchen quietly so as not to bother my parents who were in the front of the Do-nut Shop. I think Joe was afraid they would be mad at him.

Funny thing about my wreck; Jim had a similar accident in that alley on Bank Street, but at the other end, a few years before. Jim was riding his bike on Market Street and started to cross that alley when a car pulled in front of him and he went over the hood. After my incident, I never took that route through uptown again.

Even though I had been hit by a car and shelved for about three weeks, there was still some summer left. In the time without my bike, my days were spent with the television and board games. Kids came over almost everyday while I was recovering, and we played games and watched the ever present boob tube, so called because it made boobs, or dummies, out of those who watched it constantly. We watched The Price is Right, Truth or Consequences, and The Match Game. None of them was as good as the Three Stooges film fest on Saturday mornings, or the great action stories like Sky King or Sergeant Preston of the Yukon, or Roy Rogers, King of the Cowboys. Those were some fine shows that taught values without being preachy, and you could always count on the heroes being good, and not turning suddenly evil or having a dark side. George Reeves kept my interest as Superman, and I never once tried to climb on top of a building and jump off thinking I could fly.

Television in the 60's had a certain naiveté about it. Lucy and Desi never slept in the same bed, and they did not try to educate me about how Lucy got pregnant. I never questioned how she had the baby, and cameras did not follow her into the delivery room. That redhead had a great quality -- she made people laugh and forget their troubles. There were no statements about politics or social happenings. Reality TV was called the news; "Uncle" Walter Cronkite served it up with no flair, and looked right at the camera with no hidden agenda. Kids never had to sort out the difference between reality and the fantastical world of the television.

Mom finally let me go outside around the first of August. Those were the dog days of summer, and we were not rich enough to have air-conditioning. Jim and I would swelter in our concrete block room with the louvered glass windows that cranked outward for ventilation. We each had a fan that blew on us, but the air was still humid, and the little fat boy perspired profusely. Jim and I would sometimes sleep on the open ended patio which had a roof over it. That would give us an added breeze and also the freedom to wander the neighborhood in stealth after our parents went to sleep.

CHAPTER SEVEN

Hoopeston bills itself as "The Sweet Corn Capital of the World" and no one to this day has challenged that claim. With regard to farming, harvesting, processing, canning, merchandising, and shipping, the town was self-contained. Hoopeston had three food packing plants: Stokely-Van Camp, and two Joan of Arc plants ran twenty-four hours a day, seven days a week during the cornpack season; the rest of the summer they packed tomatoes, peas, kidney beans, and asparagus. American Can Company on Main Street manufactured enough cans keep the plants canning at full tilt throughout the season. Food Machinery Corporation (FMC) designed the pickers, packers, and box machines to help them get their product to market. In addition to these large commercial enterprises, there was a little known bottling company that sat about half a block from The Do-nut Shop at the corner of Penn Street and First Avenue. It, too, ran day and night, pumping out beverages like Grape Nehi and some kind of orange-flavored beverage that rivaled Orange Crush, as well as a drink called Howdy Cola. We served Howdy Cola in our shop.

Cornpack seemed to awaken the city and everybody in it from August through October. Corn was brought to the packing plants in wagons pulled by tractors. Farmers would bring their loads into the town, stopping first at the migrant camp at the south of town to be weighed. Then they would line up along First Avenue and Washington Street and wait for their turn to off-load their goods before returning to the fields.

The kids in town were fascinated by the constant parade of wagons. The smell of freshly cut corn made our mouths water. We would often go down to the plants where workers were pushing corn into a hopper and ask for handouts. The workers would give us a few ears each and we would take them home to our mothers for dinner. No corn on the planet was as sweet and juicy as the corn we got from those folks. It was fresher than anything one could buy at the grocery store. "Don't pick the corn until the water's a'boilin," was the local mantra.

Hoopeston had earned the title of "Sweet Corn Capital of the World" by canning enough corn every year to give each person in the world (not counting China) one can of corn apiece.

Hoopeston welcomed many migrant families from Texas and Mexico during the growing and harvesting seasons. The families stayed in the camps north and south of town on properties owned by the two canning companies. Joan of Arc owned the southern camp, which had formerly been a World War II prisoner of war camp. Dad had served during the war in a detachment that ferried German prisoners from Morocco to the United States, and he had brought some of the prisoners to Hoopeston. The prisoners were housed in a fenced camp surrounded by armed guards in towers. They were marched into the town during the day to rebuild the brick streets, taking up the paving bricks and putting them back down so the streets were smooth. The prisoners also worked in the fields and the factories. They were fed well and treated well. Once canning season was over in October, the prisoners would be moved to another location to help with that area. After the war most returned to their home country, although some settled in the Midwest.

The migrant workers came every spring and summer to help in the fields. The northern camp, built by Stokely-Van Camp, was constructed specifically for the families that came from near and south of the border. Workers' families stayed in these small apartments and the old prisoner barracks of Joan of Arc during their time in Hoopeston.

At the end of the season, to celebrate Labor Day and the coming end of corn pack, the Hoopeston Junior Chamber of Commerce, or Jaycee's for short, sponsored a week long celebration at McFerren Park on the western edge of town. The Jaycee's worked tirelessly all year planning the event to ensure the annual Sweet Corn Festival was one the community could be proud of. It was a kid's dream, and we all looked forward to it, even though we knew that on Tuesday following Labor Day, the new school year would start and our summer would be over.

The kids of the community were always thrilled because there would be carnival rides. The closest amusement park was Riverview in Chicago, so having a real carnival come through town was a yearlong build up. The Tilt-a-Whirl, Ferris Wheel, Merri-Mixer, Loop the Loop, and the Rocket Ride brought excitement and high blood pressure to kids of all ages. The Jaycee's provided plenty of security, and parents were able to drop their children off with a few dollars for rides and corndogs and leave them alone for a few hours, knowing they would be safe. Folks from all around came to the Sweet Corn Festival, and as the years went on, more and more attractions were added.

In addition to the midway, there were horse shows, car shows, a demolition derby, teen dances, and tents filled with food stands. Of course, the pride and joy of the festival was the sweet corn.

The canning plants provided the Jaycee's with tons of sweet corn and the delicious ears were given away with generous abandon. The Illini Supersweet was unceremoniously dumped into piles on the ground near a giant steam engine at McFerren Park. Volunteers then shucked each ear by hand. The corn was cooked in a large horse tank where the engine pumped steam into the water. After about ten minutes, the ears were taken out in baskets, turned onto a draining tray, and slathered with butter and salt. Everyone who brought a bucket, or maybe a roaster, or just held out their hands, received enough corn to fill whatever container they had brought. This went on from early evening until sunset for three days during the festival.

The Sweet Corn Festival took on even more significance when the Jaycee's added a beauty competition. They decided that having a local Miss Hoopeston to represent the town was not enough. They wanted someone to be the "National Sweet Corn Sweetheart." The lucky winner would carry the banner and represent Hoopeston and the Jaycees at events around the country. The organizers of the pageant had grandiose plans. They did not want just anyone for their competitions, they wanted the first runners up from states' Miss America Pageants to come to Hoopeston and vie for the title of National Sweet Corn Sweetheart. And they came! Beauty Queens from all over the country happily came to Hoopeston to compete in a pageant that was as rigorous as the Miss America Pageant. These young ladies stayed with respectable families in the community and were given the keys to the city. Beauties visited canneries, factories, civic functions, and attended parties all week leading up to the three day choreographed competition for the title. And, if they were lucky, one or two might get called away to compete in the Miss America Pageant. By the end of the week, the contestants knew Hoopeston was truly serious about its corn and its title as Sweet Corn Capital of the World.

Along with the beauty queen competition, the town also had a parade. The procession was open to anyone who wanted to display something, like an antique car, or who just wanted to be seen. Companies and civic organizations built floats, scout packs walked, politicians rode in cars, and horse drawn carriages rolled down the street. Cowboys on horseback strutted their stuff, the beauty queens were on display in convertibles, and high school bands from all over the state came to march in the mile-long parade. Hundreds of folks viewed the event from lawn chairs at the curb, or from rooftops along the parade route. Our family and most of our neighbors walked to the end of the block at Main Street just north of the Do-nut Shop and set up our lawn chairs early so we could see the procession. As the parade went by, we would yell at people we knew and applaud the celebrities who passed by. Of course, politicians would either get booed or wooed depending on their popularity during election years. Everyone stood and men removed their hats when each flag of a color guard passed by. The American Legion and the Veterans of Foreign Wars always led the parade, and other organizations would show their patriotism by displaying the American Flag on their floats, cars, and bicycles.

At the end of the parade came the old steam engine that the Jaycee's used to cook corn at McFerren Park, followed by a police car or fire engine to mark the end of procession. Kids often fell in line behind the parade as it wound its way into McFerren Park, smiling and waving to the crowd as they tried to get into the park for free. Sometimes it worked, depending who was manning the entry.

All in all, the week of the National Sweet Corn Festival brought recognition to the town and the Jaycees. But nothing topped the excitement kids got on the rides. My personal favorite was the Ferris Wheel. I loved the exhilaration of flying into the air and overlooking the rooftops from fifty feet up. I could see most of the town and many of the farms from there. If I was lucky, I would get stopped at the top for a while, suspended from the earth in a small car that was gently swinging back and forth. The suspension was death-defying and the closest I would come to anything remotely like jumping out of an airplane. I was not the brightest kid in town, but who would want to jump out of an airplane with a handkerchief tied to his back and hope he floated gently down from the sky? I remember seeing the landings my army action figures made, and there was no way that was going to happen to me! But the Ferris Wheel offered a chance to rise above the town safely, and I took the opportunity often. The other rides, like the Merri Mixer and the Tilt-a-Whirl, tossed me around and made me dizzy; I settled for the Ferris Wheel and its romantic view of the city and the festival.

My summers would often end on Monday afternoon, as I enjoyed my last ride of the year on the Wheel. Those last few fleeting moments in the summer sun always had me reflecting on what had happened during the summer and anticipating how things might be during the new school year.

CHAPTER EIGHT

Summers came to an end the day following The National Sweet Corn Festival. Kids gaily dressed in their new school clothes and flooded the sidewalks on their way to the three elementary schools, the junior high, and the high school in Hoopeston. Lincoln was the oldest of the elementary schools and sat at the corner of Lincoln Street and First Avenue occupying a little less than two lots, but with a huge playground across the street that filled half a block and was bound by the Chicago and Eastern Illinois Railroad on the east. Honeywell was on Honeywell Street, and it took up the entire block. It had once been the town's high school and part of the playground was on the old football field, where bleachers and light posts still remain. Maple School was the newest of the three and sat on, you guessed it, Maple Street. It took up about half a block with only one lonely little house occupying a corner of its world. School officials were not very imaginative in their naming of the schools, but rather chose the easy way and the best way for kids to remember where they went to school. No Dwight Eisenhower Elementary or Mary Hartwell Catherwood School for Hoopeston. Nope; the schools used plain ol' names from plain ol' streets.

The only exception was John Greer Junior High School. John Greer sat on an entire two block area that was bound by Main Street on the north, Penn Street on the south, Sixth Avenue on the west and Fourth Avenue on the east. John Greer Junior High had once been John Greer College, and later, John Greer High School. Apparently Hoopeston was big enough at one time to accommodate a high school and a college.

John Greer, the man, had donated over forty thousand dollars in the late nineteenth century to Hoopeston for the establishment of a college. The school originally had one building, but sometime in the 1920s, a gym was built and was attached to the original building via a tunnel. This made it possible for students to pass to classes without going outside. The

51

tunnel and the old building stood until the mid 1980s when a new school building was constructed onsite. The gymnasium is still used. Before the construction of gym which housed a large stage and the basketball court, kids played basketball in the top floor of the old building. There were unpadded poles on the sidelines, so players had to be extra careful. When times became tough and enrollment dropped off, the college became John Greer High School. In the late 1940s, the high school closed, was absorbed by the school district, and became John Greer Junior High School. At last report, it had become John Greer Elementary school. I'm not sure if there are plans to turn it into a daycare center.

John Greer, the man, had done what he intended to do, provide Hoopeston with a place to educate its youth.

In fifth grade at Lincoln Elementary school, I had one of the toughest teachers I'd ever known. Mr. Vonderheid taught me lessons that have remained with me to this day. He was from the "old school" of teaching. He drilled and drilled us like soldiers until we knew our lessons inside and out. I can do math in my head because he drilled times tables into us. Can't tell him what eleven times eleven is? Write all the times tables from one to twelve, ten times each. We started the day with times tables, we ended the day with times tables, we wrote times tables after restroom break, and we stopped birthday parties to write times tables. By the end of the year, if we did not know times tables, we stayed with him another year. No one wanted that!

Mr. V had that stern German professorial look. His hairline was receding and he combed what hair he had straight back. The glasses he wore barely fit his face, and were small and round, giving him a dictator-like guise. He would often snap his suspenders as he waited for answers to questions, and was quick with praise as well as condemnation. We feared him, and yet we loved him. No one wanted to let him down, so we worked hard in his class. At recess, he would sometimes play kickball with us, but always had someone run for him because he did not want to get his suit dirty. He spoke fluent German, and would often let go with some good words when he was frustrated with us, knowing full well we could not understand a word he said. But we got the message. He could be compassionate, but he rarely let that side of his personality show.

The one time I saw him get upset to the point of tears was in November of 1963. Novembers in Illinois were a mix of spring and winter weather. The warm days of Indian Summer often let us go to school without a coat, but by the end of the day, the weather could be cold and rainy without warning, sending us home sometimes in a freezing drizzle. School, by November, was a little long in the tooth and everyone was getting antsy for a break around Thanksgiving.

That November was like most. We had some very warm days, but the late afternoon would often bring terrible winds and thunder storms. There was always a storm on the horizon, and we got used to going into the hallway or the basement to practice our *duck and cover* skills should a tornado come. Often the drill was preceded by our principal, Mr. Keller, coming into the room and whispering something to Mr. Vonderheid, who would wait a few minutes before announcing that we were to go directly to the basement, get down on our knees facing the wall, and cover our heads with our hands.

On this particular Friday, November 22, things were different. Our class had just returned from lunch and we were getting started with our times tables. Around one o'clock, the door opened and Mr. Keller motioned to Mr. Vonderheid to come into the hall. We all knew what would happen next, as the sky outside was beginning to darken. When he stepped back into the room, Mr. V was visibly shaken. He took off his glasses, pulled a handkerchief out of his pocket and wiped his eyes. He turned to the board for a moment, took a deep breath, and then faced the class with tears streaming down his cheeks. "Class, we will be letting school out in a few minutes. You are to go directly home, or to your babysitter. Do not stop to play." We all wondered what had happened that school could be let out so early, and we were directed to go straight home. "Mr. Keller has just told me that President Kennedy has been killed this afternoon." Silence reigned over the class as we stared at Mr. V, who was struggling to keep himself composed.

Bill Gholson looked up at him and asked, "How did he die?"

"Someone shot him," was the reply. "That is really all I know. Your parents will have to cover the rest of this when you get home. Those of you who have TV will be able to watch it on the news." With that, the bell rang and the school let out one classroom at a time. The silence of all the students leaving without talking was eerie. Even when we hit the playground, there was little talk or play, as everyone did as they were told for a change, and headed home. Some of the kids cried, others were stunned. I don't think anyone knew what this meant to them, they just knew that whatever had occurred was something that was horribly wrong.

At The Do-nut Shop, Mom and Dad had pulled the TV from the living quarters and put it up on top of the counter in the corner. The place was packed, but silent, as people listened to the breaking news delivered by Walter Cronkite and the CBS broadcasters. As we sat there watching and taking in the news, the heavens opened up and rain poured out. The showers were not gentle, but rather fierce and pounding as water flooded streets and washed the pavement. The rain kept coming for days and did not stop until after President Kennedy's funeral.

A ten-year-old does not really have a perception of the huge impact the death of a president has on a nation. But for the next few days, I saw grownups cry. Mom and Dad closed the shop out of respect, they said, and we sat glued to the TV, watching every moment of coverage. People acted as though a family member had died. I remember tearing up as the drums beat the funeral cadence for the march through Washington. That sound and cadence have stayed with me in the background of my mind. It had no ruffles or flourishes, just a tender "pum pum pum, pum-pum-pum-pum, pum pum." And when John-John raised his little hand in salute as his father's casket went by, my Mom left the room. As a fifth grader, I knew that this occurrence would affect me, but the real impact of the event did not touch me until years later as a man.

School was called off for almost the entire next week. Monday was a national day of mourning and by Wednesday, we were going to be out anyway for Thanksgiving, so the school district took the three days off and we went back the following Monday. With about three weeks until Christmas break, we dove into our times tables with reckless abandon. Kids were resilient back then, and we did not have counselors to help with the trauma of the assassination, we just dealt with it by concentrating on the task at hand . . . getting up to twelve times twelve by the time we left for Christmas break in three weeks.

Mom always made us sit down on Thanksgiving weekend and make up our Christmas wish lists. I guess she gave it to Santa, or something, because we always seemed to get the majority of things that we wanted. I tried very hard to make up a list that Thanksgiving, but nothing seemed right. I settled on one thing, giving Christmas to an orphan. I have no idea how that came into my head, but it did. When Mom queried me about the list, I told her that all the other items, including a new bike, were secondary to giving another kid who was in an orphanage a chance to have a real Christmas with our family. Mom smiled, gave me a big hug and promised me she would work on it. I wondered why she had to work on it; the list was for Santa. She said that she would speak with Santa, and maybe someone who could help Santa make arrangements.

The Do-nut Shop catered to many levels of important people -- state police officers, volunteer firemen, factory workers, retail clerks, and the mayor. Even our State Senator, Tom Merritt, who lived on East Maple Street, stopped in for coffee and doughnuts. Among our clientele was a man by the name of Glenn Brasel. Glenn was an older gentleman, about six feet two inches tall, who had an air about him that everyone liked and respected. He was the local probation officer. Glenn had come into the position after retiring from teaching and coaching. He was so highly regarded, that after his death, the town named the high school athletic complex after him. According to local legend, a writer for the Danville Commercial News made a comment to Coach Brasel back in the 1920s that his football team was "nothing but a bunch of Cornjerkers." That established our high school football team's nickname, the Hoopeston Cornjerkers. Glenn liked the name, and it stuck.

Mom talked with Glenn one day in the shop and asked him how she might go about getting a child from the Vermilion County Children's Home in Danville to come for Christmas. Glenn, never one to pass up an opening, said, "Alta, you sure you want to get another one? It might do you some good to get rid of one or two for the holidays! Sure you don't want me to send them there?"

Mom smiled her toothy grin and looked at him sideways, "No, Bras, Don wants to invite one of the orphans to come visit us for the week."

"A week? Where did the boy get that idea? Is Jim on-board with this?" Mr. Brasel looked over at Dad, who was sitting on his stool next to the grill with his arms folded over his big belly.

"How can I say no? The kid doesn't really want anything else. He's getting a new coat; we might as well buy another. Little Jim is fine with it. He says it'll keep Don out of his hair." Dad always liked to do things that no one knew he did. I understand that he helped fund the slot machines in the back rooms at the VFW and American Legion during the 1950s, but no one outside those organizations knew it. Dad gave his approval to having another boy around the house for a week. As gruff as Dad seemed sometimes, he always had a soft spot for those who were not as fortunate as he; helping others out just came naturally to him and Mom.

Glenn shook his head, "All right, Alta, I'll contact the home to see if they have someone who would want to come up and spend the holidays with your family." And with that, Mr. Brasel turned up his collar and trudged out the door into the afternoon cold.

CHAPTER NINE

The weather had turned cold, and customers at The Do-nut Shop had replaced their tee shirts of summer and fall with sweatshirts and heavy coats. Shortly after Thanksgiving and the storms following President Kennedy's assassination, winter's mantel of white fell on Hoopeston as the folks settled in for winter. Winters in Central Illinois are unpredictable. They can be terribly cruel, or depending on La Nina, relatively mild. This winter, though, according to the wooly worms, was going to be a doozey. The Farmer's Almanac predicted heavy snow and very low temperatures, and when December came around, the Almanac's prophecy came true. The howling northwesterly winds brought mounds of snow and freezing temps that were so low the power outlets inside our apartment in the back of the shop froze over, even though the walls were insulated and sheltered from the wind by the Hatchery and Feed store next door. But we were comfortable in our home and in the shop where Dad had a propane forced air furnace installed. We had a very large propane tank outside the shop near the alley. This tubular reservoir served not only as gas storage, but also as a horse, a rocket ship, or any other mode of transportation we could think up for it. Later, Dad would invest in natural gas, my old steed outside would go by the wayside.

People's habits changed when Dad and Mom closed the doors for the winter. Up until the time when Old Man Winter showed up, the doors stayed open and the customers were lively and there was plenty of noise and laughter. The frigid weather forced people into mufflers, and the din in the shop decreased as they kept their coats on and just pulled their scarves down to sip their coffee. By mid-afternoon the front window panes were usually frosted over. The big picture windows of The Do-nut Shop allowed people driving or walking past to see who was at the counter. Often they would come inside and strike up a conversation with someone they knew. In the wintertime, however, with the iced up windows, all a passerby could see were silhouettes. When it was really, really cold, folks did not stop in as often, and business dropped off to just the regulars. One would think that hot doughnuts and coffee on a cold day would drive up sales, but people just did not want to go out unless they had to. Getting around in winter was difficult too, as snowplows were not very efficient and the white stuff stayed on the roads and then congealed into ice when it melted slightly. Dad would always be sure that the walk in front of the shop was shoveled and salted. Unfortunately, the salt often came into the shop on people's shoes.

The work day became a little longer, too, in winter. Each night, Dad put the stools up on the counter and swept the floors. But in winter, he also had to mop up the snow and mud and salt that had been tracked in during the day. Evening clean-ups became a family affair and included the hired help from the kitchen. On Sundays, Dad would strip the floors and then wax them, so our customers always saw a clean floor. Dad would get out the mop sometimes during the day right after lunch and clean up, then do it again that night.

Mom and Dad always had a young girl or a relative or friend working at The Do-nut Shop. The employee, usually the daughter of a family friend, doubled as a babysitter for my brother and me after school. Down through the years, these girls would be my imaginary girlfriends or sisters. Glenda Hufford was the first of the girls I remember. She was a pretty brunette with a wisp of blonde, who stood taller than Mom, but not as tall as Dad. She was the daughter of Mom's best friend, Ruth Hufford. Ruth had worked at the shop, too, for a time, but had fallen ill and died the previous year around Christmastime. Glenda took over for her mother at the shop when Aunt Ruth became too ill to work. (Jim and I called all close friends who were older, our Aunt or Uncle.) Mom loved Glenda like a daughter, sometimes mistakenly calling her "Ruth." Glenda would just smile and go on about her work, knowing what Mom had meant.

Glenda's beautiful brown eyes and winning smile were surpassed only by her inner beauty. Even though I tried to treat her as though she had cooties, she was constantly giving me the attention I wanted, while making sure I did not get the upper hand in the teasing department. I would wait until she had her hands deep in the soapy water while washing dishes, then I would sneak up behind her and untie her apron or poke her in the side to tickle her. This was usually followed by, "Donnie, you wait until I get my work done! You'll be one sad, sorry little man!" Then, with a flip of her head, she would turn back around to the sink and skulk at me out of the corner of her eye. She often let me stew after she was done, allowing me to think she would not retaliate. I knew better, though, and anxiously waited for her attack. Sometimes it would not come for days. Other times, she would wait until my back was turned and then take her soapy hands and grasp my head near the ears and hold me until I yelled for my parents. They always laughed and never admonished her. They were smart enough to know who had started the ruckus.

Dad teased the girls to no end, especially Glenda. From the girls' boyfriends to their plans for their lives, nothing was off limits to him. They were the daughters he never had, and he was "Uncle Jim." Dad was the one they went to with problems when their own fathers were not available. Dad was like the bartender who often listened and never judged. When they asked his opinion, he didn't sugar coat it. Dad often appeared gruff, but with these girls, he always took time to listen, and rarely raised his voice at them, even when they broke cups.

Glenda, Jim, Dad, Mom, and I were all working late in the shop on a Friday in the second week of December. The day had been extremely snowy, and the shop floor was a mess. Fridays were days when the grease was changed in the doughnut machine and the shop floors got a good mopping and waxing. I was tasked with putting the stools up on the counter while Mom and Glenda prepared to empty the machine. Putting the stools up on the counter upside down was no easy task for me, a little fat guy. I barely stood as high as the counter, so turning them over and putting them up onto the counter often became a wrestling match. Jim busied himself cleaning the counters and Dad was puttering in the back repairing a sink that had a blocked drain. The windows of the store were frosted heavily both inside and out, and from the street, passersby could only make out shadows. We could not see out, either, and with the sun set, there was a mysterious air about the darkened shop, which was lit by six incandescent bulbs. It was not an air of dread, but one of anticipation and excitement for me. Christmas was only a couple weeks away, and we had not decorated yet.

Off in the corner near the window, Mom and Glenda were engrossed in conversation. "How are you doing, Glen?" Mom whispered to her cleaning partner.

"Good, but it got harder this week, I think. This will be the first Christmas without Mom." Glenda was the oldest of the Hufford children and she had often taken her pay home so her Mom could buy fabric and sew clothes for her and her siblings. Mom told me that Aunt Ruth was an excellent seamstress who sewed most of her own clothes and those of her children. Mom smiled at Glenda gently, put her hand on Glenda's arm and said, "I loved your Mom very much. When she died, it left a big hole in my heart. You and Rita and the boys are family. You know I am here."

"I know, Aunt Alta. You and Uncle Jim have been so good to us. I hope you know that." Glenda seldom mentioned her father, Barney, who worked next door at Biedenkopf's Body Shop. He had taken the death of his wife very hard. "Jim and Don are like my brothers, they are too young to understand the loss and the anniversary. The season is just a little depressing."

"Well, then, we have to do something your Mom would want us to do."

"What's that?"

"She was always in charge of decorating the shop, so that's now your job!"

"I...I don't know the first thing about decorating! Where do I start?"

"Go back and tell Uncle Jim you need the Christmas decorations." And with that, Mom opened the drain plug and let the grease from the machine flow into a can. Glenda stood and looked at her with that deer-in-the-headlights look. A big smile came across her face and she leaned over and kissed Mom on the cheek and headed for the kitchen.

"Uncle Jim, Aunt Alta says you need to get the Christmas decorations."

Dad, who was sharpening the doughnut cutter, put his file down, shook his head, and sarcastically yelled at Mom. "You're letting this one do your decorations? She can hardly decorate herself!" Glenda threw a towel at him as he went through the door into the storeroom. She was beaming from ear to ear when he brought the boxes back into the kitchen. "There ya' go, Glen. Have at it!" She put her arms around his neck and gave him a big hug that almost knocked off his paper hat. She picked up the boxes and went out into the shop to lay out the contents of the box to see what she had.

After the can filled with grease, Mom set it down onto the small table next to the doughnut machine and turned her back to the large window to put the plug back into the machine. A loud knock on the window next to her made her jump, bump the table, and she almost spilled the grease. A shadowy figure sporting a large fedora trudged on towards the door and turned the knob to enter. Dressed in a long brown coat with the collar turned up and a tan scarf, the man entered, kicked the snow off his boots, and removed his hat.

"Glenn Brazel! You do that again, and you won't be eating those crippled doughnuts you like so well, you'll be crippled!" Mom shouted at him.

Braz let out a deep chuckle, "Al, you know I couldn't resist. Seeing your beautiful shape on the window, I knew you would jump pretty high. Wish they let girls play basketball when you were young, you have good reactions." He laughed heartily at his own joke.

"We'll see how you react to hot coffee in your lap! What are you doing sneaking up like that?"

"I got your boy."

Mom's eyes got real big, and she glanced quickly over to where I stood in the corner next to the grill. I was not paying attention, as I was trying to hoist a stool up onto the counter. "Don, did you hear Braz? Your Christmas wish is going to come true. We get to host a young man from the orphanage in Danville." I huffed the restaurant furniture up onto its perch, then ran around the outside of the counter to Braz.

"What's his name? Is he my age? Can we go get him today?"

Braz paused for a moment after my barrage of questions. "Larry… yes…and no." Mr. Brazel turned to Mom as Dad came out of the kitchen, "You can go get Larry Grant on Christmas Eve day, and he has to be back the following week. I think you will like him. The only thing the officials ask is that you do not push him to answer questions about his family. He really does not know anything about them. He has been at the home for quite a while. Larry is a nice boy, they tell me, and will get along with your boys quite well."

Dad looked over at me, smiled, and winked. "We'll get him Braz. Thanks for all your help with this."

"There will some extra cripples for you when you come in Monday," Mom said to him as she gave him a big hug.

"Thanks, Coach Brazel!" I yelled from behind the counter. Mr. Brazel touched the brim of his hat, turned up his collar and went out into the frozen evening.

Glenda, toting boxes of Christmas decorations, smiled. Jim and I rushed to help her with the boxes. "Looks like we'll decorate tonight after we get the chores done," she said.

It was going to be a great Christmas.

CHAPTER TEN

In the weeks that followed the news of Larry's impending visit, winter took a tighter grip on central Illinois. As the snow piled up, and the temperatures dropped, spirits were not dampened in The Do-nut Shop. Glenda had done a wonderful job decorating the place, stringing lights and simulated evergreen strands around the walls. The tree that Dad and Jim bought uptown at the Grab-It-Here grocery store on Market Street stood majestically in the corner near the large picture window. Atop the tree was a beautiful white angel that had been in the family for years. The angel shone brightly among the colored lights, multi-sized decorations, and sparkling tinsel. She peered down at the customers, who had mostly recovered from the horror of President Kennedy's assassination. Christmas music played on the AM radio perched atop the cup stand.

Mom had added her own little touch to the decorations, dangling a sprig of mistletoe from the ceiling over her seat at the doughnut machine. This was no easy task as the ceilings were well over ten feet high. Dad set up his ladder and stapled the mistletoe so it hung just right. Every male customer, and some female, gave Mom a kiss on the cheek as they came in when she was at the machine. She would respond, "Well, thank you! And a Merry Christmas to you!" Only Arnold Schuff, refused to kiss Mom. He would just pat her on the head and tell her, "That's all you will get from me this year, Tilly." He seldom referred to her as "Alta" or "Ma" or "Al" like other customers. He, instead, lovingly called her by the name she grew up with as she was passed from relative to relative after her parents' death when she was only three. Mom's parents had died in the great flu pandemic of 1914, along with Mom's younger sister, Pauline.

"So, I hear you're getting a boy from the children's home in Danville?" Schuff asked her as he took his usual seat near the grill, his coffee with cream and sugar and his two vanilla doughnuts already waiting for him.

"Sure you are up to that?" Schuff had known Mom for years and knew that she had some severe health problems, including asthma.

"Things will be fine, Schuff. Braz tells me that the young man is very well mannered, and has a great sense of humor."

"He'll need it with this family!" Schuff laughed. "Nobody teases more than Jim." Dad got a mock pained look on his face and folded his arms over his stomach.

Dad raised one eyebrow, "Schuff, I have no idea what you're talking about. I never tease anyone, just ask Glenda." Mom giggled as she thought of how Dad had put a captured turtle in the sink one day when Glenda was doing dishes. She had screamed, ran out of the kitchen, and poked Dad in the stomach. She was angry at him because she had to rewash all the dishes.

My brother and I busied ourselves cleaning our room in the back of the apartment. Larry was going to sleep in our room on a rollaway bed we had brought from Granny's house after she died. There was a lot of space in the room after we picked up everything that was scattered on the floor. Cleaning was not our forte, however, and Glenda and Mom checked on us frequently to make sure we got all the dust bunnies. At fourteen, Jim was involved in all sorts of activities from basketball to student council at school, so he was rarely in the room, and he often told Mom that the mess was mostly mine – and it was. Jim read books and studied, I busied myself with a typical ten year old's activities -- action figures, toys, and board games.

"Jim, do you think we will be able to keep Larry after Christmas?"

"He's not a puppy, goofy. He goes back to the orphanage after Christmas."

"He will be fine. He goes to school in Danville and he has friends there. Don't worry, someone will adopt him."

"But nobody has so far."

"Don't worry about it. Let's have fun with him for the week he is here." Jim picked up a pillow and threw it at me, hitting me in the face just as Glenda came in to check on us.

"Hey! You guys have to get this room cleaned up. It is Christmas Eve and you are going to Danville in a few minutes." Glenda was only three years older than Jim, but he knew that if he goofed off and did not do his share of the work, she would tell our parents. We quickly finished our task, passed Glenda's inspection, and presented ourselves to Mom and Dad to find out when we were leaving.

The shop usually closed around noon on Christmas Eve. It stayed open through the morning rush and for people to stop in and get their doughnuts for Santa on Christmas morning. Business was brisk and the laughter that filled the place warmed the faces of the customers as they braved the wintry weather. Schuff was the last one to leave. He shook Dad's hand, wished him a Merry Christmas, and headed toward the door. As he passed Mom, who was cleaning the doughnut machine, he sat down on the stool under the mistletoe. "Hey, Tilly!" He said to her, looking up at the plant of peace.

"What do you want?"

"The mistletoe, I'm under it." She walked around the machine, leaned in to Schuff, and patted him on the head.

"Have a great Christmas, Schuff." Then she put her arms around him and gave him a big hug. Dad, never one to be jealous, laughed heartily at these two friends who constantly needled each other.

Mom locked the door behind Schuff as Dad turned off the lights. The lights from the tree bathed the room in a warm glow and the music of Silent Night, sung by Bing Crosby, floated through The Do-nut Shop. Dad called Glenda out of the kitchen and told her to get her coat on; she was done for the day. She protested, saying there were still a few dishes left, but Dad told her that he would do them. He gave her a gaily wrapped package, tied with a bright red ribbon. She blushed as Dad and Mom both hugged her and wished her a Merry Christmas. Dad then hit the "No Sale" button on the cash register and pulled out a twenty dollar bill, which he handed to Glenda. "Here, get something for your family." Glenda's eyes teared up and she threw her arms around Dad. She hugged Mom, too. As she put on her coat, and started to leave, Glenda came around the counter and gave me a hug also, and then caught Jim under the mistletoe, embarrassing him thoroughly. She wished us Merry Christmas and went out into the afternoon.

"Time to go get our new kid," Dad whispered to Mom. "I'll go warm up the car."

Mom, Jim, and I put on our coats, checked the doors, and piled into the 1960 Ford Galaxy for the trip to Danville. We headed west on Penn Street and south on Route One to the county seat of Vermilion County. The usual half hour trip to Danville went slower than usual because of road conditions. The anticipation of meeting Larry and the icy roads made the trip drag. I agonized over how to greet him. Do I shake his hand? What will I say? I bombarded Mom with questions. Mom assured me that the best way was to introduce myself and wish him Merry Christmas. The rest would take care of itself.

The Vermilion County Children's Home was a large foreboding structure that sat back off the road on an estate near the north end of Danville. The structure had a creepy look to it, as though it relished in its part in people's lives. The foreboding sky was dark, and the wind had picked up, howling through the barren tree branches. As we entered the front hallway, I caught the scent of disinfectant. There were kids in the halls; others were sitting on couches and at tables. Suddenly their eyes were on us and a few had a look of anticipation on their faces.

The door to the office squeaked as we opened it, startling the lady sitting at a desk behind a large counter. "May I help you?" she queried with a gravelly voice.

Mom cleared her throat, took off her gloves, and spoke, "We're the Shields' from Hoopeston and we are here for Larry Grant."

The lady turned to a large console with a microphone on it, pushed the button and yelled, "Larry Grant! Get your things and come to the office!" She probably could have been heard without the sound system. The kids outside the office looked up, smiled, and shouted to Larry as he came into the room, "Have a great time Larry! Merry Christmas!" They seemed genuinely cheerful that Larry was escaping for the holiday.

Larry stood about my height, had blonde hair, a big toothy grin, and was full of enthusiasm. As he walked toward us there was a joyful bounce in his step. The lady behind the desk introduced Larry to us and was full of nice things to say about him. He blushed as she went on about how well behaved he was, how he was such a good student, and how everyone at the home loved him. She was happy that Larry was going to spend Christmas with us. Larry thanked the lady, whom he called Mrs. G, and hugged her.

Larry and I sat in the back seat in silence, looking at each other. Jim broke the ice by asking Larry about his favorite baseball team. When Larry answered, "the Cardinals," we immediately started ribbing him. He realized he was with a bunch of Cubs fans, and started giving it right back to us. We laughed and talked sports all the way back to Hoopeston. From then on, we talked about all possible subjects, except for Larry's past.

When we arrived back at home, Larry seemed disappointed that we lived in an apartment. The look on his face said he thought we lived in a house, but he was polite enough not to say anything. Jim and I took him to our room in the back, and set him up with a place to put his suitcase and coat. Since it was early evening by the time we got home, Mom made us her usual Christmas Eve dinner of cheese sandwiches and chili. We boys ate at the counter, like customers, while Mom and Dad disappeared to the apartment to wrap presents.

"You guys live in the back of the restaurant?" Larry asked with wonder.

"We have always lived here, once you get past the kitchen, it is just like any other house," Jim replied. "And the storeroom is a great place to play. We play basketball in there sometimes, and wiffle ball."

"Do you like the place where you live?" I asked. Jim shot me a look that said I should shut up.

"It's okay, I guess," Larry responded. "I really have never lived anywhere else that I can remember. I have a lot of brothers and sisters there, but nowhere really that I can go just to be alone. You guys have the storeroom, or can go to your bedroom, but I pretty much always have someone around. This trip is something I've been looking forward to." He smiled and crushed some crackers into his chili.

"I've been looking forward to it, too," I assured him. Larry looked at me, stuck out his hand and we shook on being friends.

Mom and Dad came out from the kitchen and put their stools down opposite ours. "Guys it is Christmas Eve, and since we have a new addition to our family this year, I thought we should do something different." Our family did not go to church on Christmas Eve, so Jim and I looked at each other quizzically. Our routine was to watch A Christmas Carol on TV, then put out doughnuts and milk for Santa before turning in for the night. "Tonight is a good night to start new things, so we will begin a new tradition of playing board games. Family Board Night, we'll call it!" And with that, Mom pulled out a stack of games: Monopoly, Life, Candyland, Sorry, Checkers, all the games we had were before us. Jim and Dad chose Checkers; Mom, Larry, and I chose Sorry. We played those games until almost midnight, laughing and teasing, and having a great time. It did not take Larry long to become comfortable with our family, and he quickly learned how to tease and be teased.

At midnight, our parents called an end to Family Board Night, and we boys headed for bed. "Hey! Aren't you forgetting something?" Dad called after us. He reached under the counter and brought out a tray of doughnuts. "Don't forget to leave something for Santa!" Larry, not knowing what to do, stood back while Jim and I each chose two doughnuts and put them on a plate. "Come on, son, choose the doughnuts you want

Santa to have and put them on the plate," Dad instructed. Larry picked two fat doughnuts and put them in the center of the plate.

"Will Santa eat those?"

"Either he will, or his elves will get a snack, too!" Dad laughed. Now, scoot! Off to bed, all of you!"

We went over to Mom and gave her a big hug. When it came Larry's turn, he put his arms around her. "Thanks, Mrs. Shields," he said quietly.

"For the next week, I'm Mom, Larry." Larry grinned widely as we went to bed and waited for Santa.

The three of us all woke before dawn, and Jim led the way as we sneaked out to the shop to find the doughnuts had all been eaten, the milk had been drunk, and the tree was surrounded by presents. Larry was apprehensive, though, as he did not know if there would be any presents under the tree for him. We were not allowed to touch any of the presents until Mom and Dad had their coffee and came out to join us. Larry's fears were soon put to rest as there were plenty of presents under the tree for everyone. Mom and Dad had taken great care to be sure we all had the same number of presents. I was happy with my best present -- seeing Larry's joy as he unwrapped his gifts.

The rest of the week flew by quickly as we spent our time either outside playing in the snow or inside playing with our Christmas presents. Mom took us to McFerren Park one day to play on the ice. The Lagoon in the middle of the park froze in the winter and there were large areas for ice skating. One area was for guys who wanted to play hockey; the other was for people who wanted to just glide along. I had no idea how to skate, but Larry borrowed skates from one of the other kids, and he turned out to be a miracle on ice. He could do loops and figure eights and could even skate backwards! By the end of week, we were fast friends and did not want to separate, but we knew that Larry he had to go home to Danville.

The drive back to the children's home was much quieter than the one we had taken a week earlier. Larry and I hardly looked at each other, let alone talked. We stared out of our respective windows and commented only on the passing landscape, and the times we'd had together. When we reached Danville, Larry and I both had tears in our eyes. We were only ten and had known each other only a short time, but we had become brothers. Larry and I held hands as we trudged silently up the walk behind Mom and Dad. At the door of the orphanage, we were faced with the sad task of saying goodbye.

"Thanks for having me this week." Larry said, clutching at both Mom and Dad. Dad fought back some tears and was trying to be strong, but Mom let it all out and began to cry. Larry turned to me, dropped his bag, and wrapped his arms around my neck. "You're a good brother."

"Yeah, you, too. We'll see each other soon." As Larry walked into his home, several kids ran to help him with his bags of clothes and presents. With a nod, he looked back over his shoulder and smiled at us. I never saw him again.

CHAPTER ELEVEN

After Christmas break, I returned to school the first week in January. It was 1964, and although Mr. Vonderheid's fifth grade class continued to practice times tables, and we had also moved on to division, something slightly more complicated because it requires backward thinking. I had trouble at first with division as I could barely think forward. One really has to know times tables in order to understand the complexities of division, which is why Mr. V was so adamant about us learning them so we would not have to constantly refer back to printed tables and charts.

As the seasons changed and the weather began to warm, bicycles appeared once again in our neighborhood. My parents had blessed me with a new bike at Christmas, but the cold had prevented me from getting much use out of it. But now, with my new found freedom on my bike, I was able to expand my circle of friends to those who lived across town. The two-wheeled wonder opened new vistas for me, and I would ride near and far on the pretense of going to the library. I vowed to myself, however, to avoid the uptown alleys as I sallied forth to play with my friends at their houses. Mom always wanted to know where I was, and I, at all times, told her where I was going. She would surreptitiously check on me through her "mom network," or make me call her when I got to my destination.

Hoopeston had some interesting sights to see. There was the five story Wildon Building, the lagoon at McFerren Park, and a large open ditch that cut across the town on the southwest side from about Maple Street and Third Avenue all the way out of town. The ditch was the receptacle for copious amounts of waste from the homes and factories on the south side of town. There was a distinctive smell that emanated from it, a cross between beans and human offal. Appropriately, the locals called it "The Stink Ditch."

The Sweet Corn Capitol of the World was also known for being the worst smelling town in central Illinois. But The Stink Ditch was not responsible for all of the smell. Hoopeston also had two cattle pens: one on the west edge of town and one on the south edge. The cattle pens were exactly what the name implies . . . a place where cattle were penned. But there were hundreds of head of cattle. I don't know why ranchers count just the heads; isn't the rest of the body there, too? Semi-truck loads of cattle would come into Hoopeston and be put in these pens to be fattened up for slaughter. Cattle ranches were often combined with farming in East Central Illinois, but these two places were specifically for auctions, breeding, fattening, and then transporting. The Norfolk and Western Railroad even put in a set of tracks to the cattle pens out on the west side, so the cattle could be put into train cars and shipped to slaughter houses The summer humidity only exacerbated the thick stench. The only relief Hoopeston residents had was when winds blew in from the north and carried the foul odor away from town.

My best buddy during the last part of fifth grade was Roger. Roger's dad was a mechanic, so we often watched him work on cars in the garage next door to The Do-nut Shop. Kids have a way of finding each other and forming friendships quickly and Roger and I met when he and his father came into the shop one day. Before we knew it, Roger and I were making plans to get together. We quickly found we had a great deal in common and our spring and summer were filled with bike rides, sleepovers, and backyard camp outs.

Roger's brown hair was cropped close to his scalp, especially around his large ears. He was not bald, but his dad certainly had Sarge York, one of the many local barbers, get close with the clippers. Roger probably needed some orthodontics, but that was for kids whose parents had a lot of money. He had a great laugh, which he used often, and an imagination that would often lead us too close to the line we knew not to cross.

My imagination matched Roger's and I loved to laugh, too. Give me a Red Skelton or Bill Cosby record, and I was set for quite a while. Records were made of vinyl back then, and I played them on a contraption called a record player. I used it often for Red and Bill, and I could usually recite their routines word for word within a short time. Reading was something I did little of, unless Superman, Batman, and the Legion of Superheroes count.

Because of school, Roger and I could only get together on Saturdays or school holidays. And on Easter vacation, we spent more time at each other's houses than we did with our own families. One day in early April, I got ready to ride to Roger's house early in the morning. I had my normal breakfast of a half dozen doughnuts with a cup of coffee. Yes, I drank coffee when I was young. Dad always made me drink it black, no sugar. He said if I was going to drink coffee, I was going to drink it as the good Lord had intended. Dad said that if it was meant to have cream and sugar, then cows would have one udder for coffee and eat sugar plants. Roger would have had his usual breakfast of Sugar Smacks with a dash of milk, or toast with peanut butter, and maybe a slice of bologna.

I told Mom I was going to Roger's and headed out the door. Mom gave me her usual warning about being careful and looking both ways.

"Donnie, you stay out of that Stink Ditch when you go to Roger's!" She always worried that one of us would fall into the dreaded Stink Ditch, and she knew it was inevitable that Roger and I would eventually end up over there throwing rocks into it. Roger lived right next to The Stink Ditch.

"Sure, Mom," I yelled, and pedaled down the sidewalk.

At Roger's house, we plopped down in front of the old Motorola and began watching Ray Raynor and Bozo's Circus on Channel 9 from Chicago. Suddenly, we heard the sounds of men and machines. We ran to the back door to investigate.

There, in back of Roger's house, was a brand new Caterpillar bulldozer going up and down the bank of The Stink Ditch! Behind it was a group of men with a crane attached to another bulldozer. Hanging from the boom and chain was a large cement tile that was being placed into the ditch. We hopped on our bikes, and rode furiously to the Second Avenue Bridge for a better look. But there was no bridge – and no Stink Ditch!

On that day, in front of our eyes, our hometown came of age. No longer would we have a Stink Ditch, but our mothers would have greater worries. Civilization had come to us. Roger and I looked at each other and wondered what was next, dial telephones?

We watched all day as that bulldozer and crane and those men laid pipe. It was mesmerizing! Up and down, the dozer went, clearing the debris from the banks and making the ditch seem as though it had perfect sides. The crane lifted a large piece of pipe, so big that one could drive a Volkswagen through it, and laid it in the ditch. Another dozer gently pushed the pipe into position, and another filled in the ditch behind it. We watched in awe as our beloved Stink Ditch was transformed into a modern sewer.

I arrived home that night as the street lights were coming on. Mom, Dad, and Jim were in the kitchen having dinner. They had set a place, but started without me since they knew I would be late. The ride from Roger's house to ours was about fifteen minutes, and Roger's Mom had called to let Mom know I was on my way. There was very little banter around the table as I walked in, and I got the feeling that I had just missed something. I was uneasy, out of place, and my first thought was that Jim had done something bad, but when all their eyes shifted to me, I immediately began to protest. "I can explain . . ."

"Explain, what?" Dad focused fully on me, now, but his eyes did not have anger in them. Instead, they had more of a "Gotcha!" look as his eyebrows raised and he began to smirk. Mom and Jim wiggled in their seats so they could get a better view of the show that was about to begin. "Come around here, Don, so I can get a better look at you." I walked tentatively around the table and stood next to Dad as Jim and Mom put down their utensils, put their elbows on the table, and rested their heads in their hands, covering their mouths.

"Son, I have been thinking about all this riding around to Roger's house at the end of town, and the other places you have been going," he paused to let it sink in. I could feel something in my stomach begin to turn. He was going to take my bike away! I tried not to let it happen, but my lip began to quiver.

"Dad, look what you've done. You got him all worked up, just tell him." Mom said while holding her napkin in front of her face. A million thoughts raced through my head. What could this be that he was so serious? He gently folded his napkin and laid it on the table.

"Come over here, son. Sit on ol' Dad's lap." Whenever he said that, it usually was a prelude to a spanking. I did so tentatively. I could tell he was relishing in the power of suspense. "You know I love you, right? And you know I want you be happy?"

"Oh boy, are we getting a puppy!" I yelled out. But his face told me no. I stopped all the celebrating and said calmly, "Yes, Dad, I love you, too." I could feel the lip quiver again.

"Well, we can't live here anymore," he trailed off, "because, we're moving to a new house!"

I was dumbfounded. Never did I ever think that we would have a house. "Will it have a yard?" I blurted.

"Yes, a big yard."

"Are we getting animals? Can I have a pony?"

He laughed, "No, it won't be that big, it's still in town, out on West Penn Street across from McFerren Park."

"What about the shop? What will happen to this place?"

"We'll have a new shop. We start remodeling next week out there. You and Jim will have a room, but you will still have to share."

We did not care; we were going to move to a real house! We could say goodbye to the apartment, and the back alley would be exchanged for a real yard with real grass. Jim was going to be fifteen and I was nearing eleven. Our parents thought we were embarrassed to bring our friends over. Nothing could be further from the truth! Our friends never made fun of us, never said we should play at their house. They loved having doughnuts for a snack when they came to play. We usually ended up playing in the restaurant after it closed and the counters and tables and the storeroom offered great places to play hide and seek, board games, or just about anything else we could think up.

So, the spring of 1964 brought about many changes both in our town and in our lives. Dad worked hard during the afternoons and evenings getting the new Do-Nut Shop built. We saw the conversion from bottled pop to a soda machine, and Dad installed a dishwasher. Glenda did not make the move with us as she had already graduated from high school, but a new girl, Becky, was going to take her place. The new shop was a block off Route One, the main thoroughfare that took traffic past Hoopeston, and three blocks from John Greer Junior High. The old doughnut machine took its place in the corner of the new shop and the behemoth continued its never ending task of making the delights that all of Hoopeston loved.

CHAPTER TWELVE

The new chapter of our lives started in May of 1964 when we moved to West Penn Street. The new Do-nut Shop was our converted two car garage that Dad had remodeled, and he had cleared an adjoining lot for customer parking. That left the entire side yard next to our house vacant. It was perfect for our games of wiffle ball, touch football, and flashlight tag, and made a great place for us to watch the events unfold during the Sweet Corn Festival and Fourth of July celebration at McFerren Park. We were on the west edge of town, just two miles from the pungent cattle pens on Route 9. After a while, we got used to it. Until I left for college in 1975, this was home.

My parents' good friends, the Barkers, and their two sons lived a block away, and my Mom's friend, Eleanor Knoll, and her kids, Greg, Randy, and Cynthia lived across from the Barkers. Don and Frank Smith lived behind us across the alley. There was always someone to play with and every home had a big yard. For tag and water fights, we used the entire two block area because there were no fences, just open yards to run through.

We settled nicely into our new digs and became accustomed to living in the house, a single story stucco, painted white with a gray foundation. It had a basement that was functional, but hardly suited to a remodel into a family room. There was an old coal chute and coal room near the furnace. We shoveled coal into the furnace on winter days for the first several years after moving in. There was a closed-in, unheated front porch, a living room and dining room, and a kitchen with a breakfast nook. The floors were beautiful hardwood with a high patina on them. Jim and I had the back bedroom, which measured twelve by twelve, and had one window in it. It had two windows before Dad remodeled the garage into the shop, but one window was covered, so we had to settle for one double hung window that opened toward the big side yard and the parking lot. We shared the only closet in our room. The house had only one bathroom for the four of us, but when there was a conflict, we made do with the half bath in the restaurant. Mom and Dad occupied the other bedroom at the front of the house. All in all, there probably was less space than we had on First Avenue, but the arrangement of the rooms and the large side yard made it seem like a castle.

Dad did not believe in advertising a great deal. He thought that if he and Mom served a good product and offered a cheery atmosphere, then word would spread and the customers would come. The publisher of the Hoopeston Chronicle Herald ran a story about the move, and before long, business was better than ever. Dad and Mom even extended the shop's hours to include Saturday mornings. Due to a sign painter's error, The Do-nut Shop became The Do-nut Shoppe. Dad and Mom didn't mind, and the sign stayed.

After the move, our old shop was sold to Davis Sheet Metal. Buzz Davis gutted it and used the wide open space for tooling metal ductwork and various other metal works.

Jim entered high school in the fall, and I remained at Lincoln Elementary for one more year, getting Mr. Haughee as a teacher. In such a small town, Jim and I often had the same teachers as we went through school. We always enjoyed our teachers and not one ever compared me to my older brother. Jim was a much better student than I. He was in the National Honor Society and I was nowhere near smart enough for that club! I was just "too darn social," according to Mrs. Mitchell, who taught us both English in junior high. She also knew us well since we were neighbors at the original Do-nut Shop; her husband was Mitch, the proprietor of the hatchery and feed store next to us. She and Mitch would sometimes go out with Mom and Dad to the local VFW hall in the evenings for drinks. She didn't cut us any slack, however, and would not allow us any wiggle room when it came to our school work.

Sixth grade was a transition year for me. That was when I began to realize that I loved to listen to others talk, that I could easily make people laugh, and people liked to be around me. I had begun to entertain in Mrs. Stark's second grade with my Three Stooges puppets, but it wasn't until the sixth grade that I learned that I was popular and respected. I also experienced my first love, with Sarah. Being "boyfriend and girlfriend" in the sixth grade in 1965 was not very complicated. We talked on the phone, sent notes across the room in school, did some hand holding, but nothing more. We went to a few boy/girl parties, but we mostly sat, listened to music, and stared at each other, girls on one side of the room – boys on the other. Sarah was a little taller than I and we did try to dance a few times, but I had two left feet. Since we rarely saw each other outside of school, my first love experience eventually ebbed to friendship.

Our principal, Mr. Keller, was a great guy: Tall and straight with thick black hair which he combed back. Mr. Keller was a handsome figure of a man and he could have been in the movies. He would have been a great leading man or a kind, but tough sheriff in an action Western. Mr. Keller was gentle and spoke to students easily with that deep, broadcaster voice of his. When it rose to the point of shouting, we knew his paddle was soon to be used on someone's backside. I tried to avoid the paddle, but was not successful.

Apparently my teachers thought I had matured enough to be Captain of the Safety Patrol. Safety Patrol members wore special belts with a strap that looped over one shoulder, across the chest, and then attached to the belt. We were endowed with special powers to police the school grounds and crosswalks. As Captain, I was responsible for being sure the main doors to the school were protected from terrorists, like lower classmen who wanted to see teachers before the start of the day. I also had to traverse the block and inspect the posts to be sure they were manned by guards.

Mr. Keller had one hard and fast rule during winter: No Snowball Throwing on School Grounds. If a member of the Safety Patrol saw an infraction, we were to report the perpetrator, who would then receive a swat from Mr. Keller's paddle. One morning, after a heavy snowstorm, Mr. Keller walked out to the playground to make sure all was in order. I was feeling lively because I had biked the mile to get there early to man the door. As he walked by, something came over me and I picked up a snowball and threw it at him when he was just a few feet past me. Without flinching, he turned toward me and calmly pronounced, "We'll talk later about that." His voice did not express anger, but his eyes narrowed and I knew immediately that he meant business. He went to his customary place in the middle of the playground and blew his whistle for the students to assemble by classroom at the flagpole. Not many of my friends had seen what I had done, but word spread quickly. Mr. Keller led the school in the Pledge of Allegiance as usual, then he announced, "The sixth grade will go to the chorus room for a meeting." I had a feeling in the pit of my stomach that leapt into my throat. I suddenly remembered that my father had told me that if I got into trouble at school, I would get double the punishment at home.

I held the doors as the students filed past me into the building. The younger kids took little notice of me, but kids from the fourth grade and up looked at me as if I was going to the gallows. They had that somber, sorrowful look that said, "You poor devil." Some of my friends shook their heads, and one or two snickered as they passed. The sixth graders went to the basement and filed into seats in the music room; I was the last to enter and I closed the door. Mr. Keller was already at the front of the room and his paddle was lying on the desk. He read off a list of names, "Butch, Jack, Roger, Bill, and Bob, please come to the front." He did not read off my name! What relief! Each of the boys went forward and was told that he had been seen throwing snowballs and would receive a swat. Each took their turn putting their hands on the desk and leaning over and taking the position. The air whistled as the paddle went through it and made contact with a resounding slap against the trousers of each criminal. When all had taken their whacks, Mr. Keller told the boys to return to their seats.

My elation was replaced with dread as Mr. Keller said, "Don Shields, please come up front." I could feel my cheeks redden and my ears begin to tingle; I walked unsteadily to the front. "Mr. Shields, your snowball hit me, and for that you will receive two swats. You know the position." I glanced at his face and at the paddle in his hands. As I placed my hands on the desk and leaned over, I caught the eye of my friend, Debbie, and tried not to cry. The slap of the paddle against my rump sent a sharp tingling up my body, and before I could recover, there was another whack. I could feel the tears well up in my eyes, but managed to hold back the spill. The paddle didn't really hurt bad enough to cry about it, but it was humiliating and I had disappointed our Principal. I knew I would never do anything to warrant a swat ever again. The kids all kept still until Mr. Keller excused them. He held me back.

After the others had left the room, Mr. Keller turned to me and said, "Don, you are in a position of importance and it was imperative that I punish you more harshly. Do you understand?"

I didn't really, but I acknowledged him with a nod and a "Yes, sir."

"Tomorrow, you go back to your post. But this afternoon, I will have Don Smith take over for you." I left the room and went back to class. As I walked in, things were eerily quiet. No one said anything to me; Debbie just looked at me across the room and smiled. Word got around that Mr. Keller was not afraid to use his paddle. We all had great respect for him from that day on. Nobody threw snowballs at school for the rest of the winter.

The end of the school day, however, brought new anxiety as I knew I had to go home and face Dad. I waited for Don Smith so we could ride home together on our bikes. As we rode, we talked about how to handle the matter. "Should I tell him?" I asked Don.

"How is he going to find out, if you don't tell him?" Don replied.

"I don't know, but I should tell him. It could be worse for me if I don't and he finds out later."

"I would take my chances," Don advised, "he may never find out."

I was torn because I knew that many teachers came into The Do-nut Shoppe before school and surely they would spill their guts. I made up my mind to play it by ear. If Dad brought up the matter, I would tell him. If he didn't, I wouldn't, and would just take my chances. Trying my best to not draw attention to myself, I slipped in the back door and yelled that I was home.

"Come out here," yelled my father in what appeared to be a happy tone.

I walked out from behind the wall that separated the front of the shop from the kitchen and found both my parents sitting at the counter having coffee. "Come around here," Mom instructed. That old familiar feeling crept into my stomach again. "How was your day?"

"Fine. The bike ride was a little cold, though." I glanced at her and then at Dad. Neither of them seemed angry. Maybe I was home free!

"Anything special happen today?" Dad was now standing and fingering his belt. I knew the jig was up, so I spilled my guts.

"What have I always told you about getting into trouble at school?" he asked, removing his belt. I immediately bent over a stool and felt the burn of the belt as it contacted my hiney. That was the last time my father ever punished me corporally. I decided right then and there that I would not get into trouble again. I saw that he did not want to give me the belt, but he had given his word about the punishment for misbehaving at school, and he had to carry it out. And this time, I actually understood.

Right after the first of the year, my favorite sports season, basketball, started. Mr. Haughee coached the team and everyone who tried out made the team. We practiced after school and on Saturday mornings, and we played games at Honeywell School against their sixth graders. I was not very good, but I enjoyed being with my friends and learning new things. Mr. Haughee made it fun and the players worked hard. But basketball was not my sport, and after sixth grade, I did not make the team again. This did not quell my enthusiasm, however, and I spent many nights in the stands at games and listening to games on the radio. My love of the game would lead me to a thirty year career coaching high school basketball.

Chapter Thirteen

At the end of sixth grade, school let out for the summer five days late due to snow days and tornado days when the schools closed. All of us, including the teachers, were antsy to get out and start summer. I had signed up for Little League baseball and we had begun practice in early May. By the end of the school year, we had already been playing other teams for a week.

I played for Silver Brothers Construction. My brother, Jim, was our coach. He had been an outstanding player all through his years in Little League and Pony League, but Hoopeston did not have baseball in the high school, so he did not get a chance to go on and play. Jim spent some time in American Legion ball, and then turned to getting a job and helping out our team. I had always wanted to pitch, but I had no control whatsoever and couldn't run worth a dang, either. So Jim assigned me to first base. All I had to do was learn to catch the ball and maybe throw it to second base if the batter got past me. Jim spent countless hours trying to teach me to bat and was somewhat successful at it. I hit my share of homeruns, but had to hit it long just to get to first base.

The Hoopeston Little League was a great learning experience. The league divided the boys up between ten teams and tried to make them as balanced as possible, given the players' ability. This did not always mean the teams were equal; kids grew and developed during the summer and so did the teams. But it was great fun and we had an excellent ballpark for such a small town.

Little League games were played at Vermilion Field, named after John Deere Vermilion Works, which built the field next door to their factory on North Sixth Avenue, just across the Norfolk and Western Railroad tracks that ran east and west through town. The factory was running full bore during baseball season, and the smell of smelting permeated the air. The sound of molten steel being poured into the casts for tractors and combines often drowned out the crowd noise of parents and other spectators. Trains passed by the field twice each evening; one going east, the other, west. They always blew their whistles at the Sixth Avenue crossing next to the ballpark, and this sometimes disrupted the games as players jumped when they heard the loud noise. Vermilion Field was our *Field of Dreams* and it was well kept and very professional looking with its grass infield, pressbox, and concrete dugouts, which were actually dug into the ground. Many leaguers wanted to not only play on that awesome field, they also wanted to be the one to take care of it. The job of groundskeeper was coveted, because the caretaker not only mowed the grass, lined the field, and cleaned up, he also got to announce the games over the public address system, like a big league public address man, keep score, and recount the games with his own byline for the Chronicle-Herald. Jim was able to do all that and coach a team as well.

It took me a long time to become a good batter and at first, I often struck out. With help from Jim, and Charlie Peterson, a man who walked on crutches because of polio, and who had great knowledge of baseball, I learned to not just hit it to right, but to go with the pitch and hit it where it needed to be hit. Trying too hard had been my problem, and as soon as I let the game come to me, I became a better hitter.

Mom often helped in the concession stand or sat in the bleachers next to the dugout. She was not very vocal, but rather sat and watched and provided encouragement to everyone on the field. She loved to watch the games, and only missed one if she was scheduled to work in the concession stand. Even then, she would watch out of the concession window as the game progressed. Dad preferred to sit in his old car next to the railroad tracks just off the left field wall. Occasionally he would lean on the back fence, but mostly he sat in his old, two-toned blue 1953 Chevy we called his "fishing car" and watched the game from there. Dad was not at all antisocial, but he liked to have a beer in the evening while he watched, and he could not very well do that in the stands. There were other parents who came to the field after they'd had a few, but Dad did not want any kids to see him with a beer in his hand. We knew Dad was paying attention, though, because he blew the car horn every time Silver Brothers scored or had a good play. He sounded it extra long when I hit a homerun.

The kids who played were all friends, but rivalry was inevitable. Butch Drollinger, Fred Sharon, Dick Rulison, Derek Baird, Mick Sille, Sid Deer, and Don Smith were all excellent players on different teams. The competition was furious during the summer and we would rib each other, but were never cruel or demeaning. And when the game was over, it was over. We would all get together on week-ends or during the afternoons on open sandlots and play all day. We made our own fun. Then we would go home, rest, and come back to Vermilion Field for the evening game.

Butch was by far the best baseball player among us. He could hit a ball for what seemed like a mile and throw with accuracy from behind the plate, where he caught, to second base like he was throwing a ball on a rope. A man among men, Butch was the one we all wanted to be, and who we measured ourselves against. While some of the boys had a little peach fuzz on their chins, others, like me, had none. But Butch was sporting a five o'clock shadow and talking with a deep voice, sounding like a grown man. We often forgot he was our age and treated him with the respect a man who could rip your arm off deserved. Butch played for Burton Motors, a team that seemed to be stacked every year. Frank Longfellow, their coach, was really good at teaching fundamentals and getting the boys to excel. It did not hurt that they had Butch, the best player in the league.

Silver Brothers and Burton Motors fought their way to the top of the league in the summer of 1965, and met in the championship game at the end of the season. We had Mike Dean, a lanky pitcher who did not look as talented as he was, and Burton Motors had Fred Sharon, a hard throwing right hander who was fast on the mound and the base paths. After a week of rain, the final game of the season would be played on a hot, steamy, Saturday afternoon in early August. It was the kind of day that made a person feel as though they were breathing through a soaked sponge. Cornpack was just starting up and the sticky, sweet smell of corn juice drifted in from Stokely-Van Camp Canning Company just east of the ball field, and tanker trucks sprayed the excess cooking water on the field across the road. Corn juice, cattle dung, and molten steel all mixed in the hot afternoon air, making us dizzy and slightly nauseous.

The seven inning game was just what a championship was supposed to be -- difficult for both teams to win. Every at bat was a struggle as the pitchers threw to determined batters, who seldom made contact with the ball. As the afternoon wore on and the sun began to sink low, Silver Brothers took a slim two run lead, thanks to some nifty base running and an error by Rulison. Burton Motors fans crowded the third base line bleachers and stood three deep next to the chain link fence as their team came to bat in the bottom of the seventh. The lower part of the order was due up, and the crowd hoped someone could get the game moving.

Dean's uniform was soaked with sweat as he stood on the mound; his arm hung at his side. The long, lean pitcher had tossed six innings, and the heat, humidity, and overpowering stench made him woozy as he looked in to the first batter. George McCormick had struck out in the number nine spot three times; this was to be no different with Dean firing three pitches by him. Silver Brothers' pitcher dispatched the next batter and the crowd began to move to their cars. Burton Motors desperately needed to get Drollinger to the plate. Glenn Richey, the lead-off hitter for Burton Motors, had not had so much as a swing against Dean all day, but he lined a single on the second pitch he saw. Roger, my buddy, worked the count to 3-2, and then he, too, coaxed a seeing-eye hit that sent Richey to third and brought Drollinger to the plate.

With two outs and two runners on base, all Drollinger had to do was hit a homerun. Surely we would walk him; he was the most dangerous man in the league, our equivalent of Babe Ruth. Jim went out to the mound and spoke to Dean and Don Smith, his battery mate. Dean shook his head in an affirmation, wiped his mouth, and kicked at the dirt as Jim went back to the dugout and Don squatted behind home plate. Drollinger dug in at the plate and smiled out at Dean, trying to show little emotion, but everyone knew what was on his mind. The lanky pitcher heaved the first pitch and Butch took it for a strike. Parents cried out that the ball appeared to them to be well out of the strike zone. The next pitch was at the letters and the umpire called it a strike. People began to come back from the parking lot, and even Dad took up his space leaning against the fence in left field and clapped his hands. Mike had a 0-2 count on Butch and thought he might be able to get him to chase one wide.

Dean toed the rubber, rocked back, and let loose with a grunt as he launched the ball toward the plate. Butch took a short step forward and brought his hands through, reaching way out on the outside of the plate for the ball as it spun toward him. The crowd took a collective breath and held it as Drollinger made contact with the ball. As the ball cleared the back fence, it was still rising. It flew over the tracks, and hit a large gas tank that stood almost two blocks away. The spectators were wild with awe and excitement. Butch had not only beaten us; he had accomplished the same feat my brother had years earlier.

As we trudged off the field in defeat, Jim put his arm around me, something he rarely did. "In a couple weeks, you'll be a teenager, little brother. There will be lots of new things coming your way in junior high." I looked up at him and smiled with anticipation.

Mom was waiting near the dugout when it was time to leave, and amazingly, so was Dad. He usually got into the car and left without a word, but today he came to the dugout and put his arm around my shoulder. No words passed between us, but we were communicating. We were all disappointed that our team had lost and there was nothing to say. Mom left with Jim while Dad and I rode home together in his fishing car.

CHAPTER FOURTEEN

The day I became a teenager was also my first day at John Greer Junior High School. Originally built as a college, John Greer's grand history gave it a special reverence in our town, and the building was meticulously maintained. It was three stories tall and had a full basement. The rooms had thirteen foot ceilings and double hung windows that opened from both the top and the bottom. The floors were oiled wood which shined at the beginning of every day.

Our house was just a few blocks from the school, and I could see it as I walked with the Smith boys, Frank and Don. When we got to the school ground, kids were everywhere! Each year, the junior high school took in all the former sixth graders from the town's three elementary schools to begin seventh grade. All the kids I knew from Lincoln sixth grade were there, and so were the sixth graders from Honeywell and Maple Schools, most of whom I'd never met. Students who had attended the same school for the past six years found themselves thrown together with kids they hadn't known before. Would our old friends still be our friends? Would we take the same classes? That first day was overwhelming.

Junior high was vastly different than grade school, where students stayed with the same teacher the whole day. Here, we had a different teacher for each subject. They were all considered experts in their field and were determined to drill their subject matter into our little heads. We no longer had the freedom to fidget or pout like we did in grade school. We sat in nice little rows with our feet out of the aisles, we opened our books on command, and we wrote or read when we were told to do so. The lessons were tough, and our teachers displayed varying degrees of rigidity.

I was fortunate, however, to take the best classes, which turned out to be fun and they shaped my future life -- English, physical education, shop, and music. The instructors who taught these classes were mostly young, hip, and enthusiastic. Mrs. Mitchell, our friend and former neighbor, was my English teacher. She was an excellent instructor and I adored her. But she showed me no favoritism, in fact, quite the opposite. She assigned me to a seat in the front row, smack in the center, where I could get away with nothing. Mrs. Mitchell had a wonderful sense of humor and laughed easily, but she was a daunting task master when it came to grammar. She relentlessly drubbed into us the foundations of language, yet allowed us leeway to express ourselves when it came to writing, as long as we adhered to the rules of Warriner's English Grammar and Composition.

Mrs. Mitchell also the sponsored the Bell Club, which held daily sock hops during lunch break so students could blow off some steam before returning to afternoon classes. Everybody loved the sock hops! Kids who usually had their lunch at the Do-Nut Shoppe would often have their parents call in their lunch order, so it would be ready when they arrived. They would race to the shop when the lunch bell rang, and Mom and Dad would have their lunches ready. Then they would wolf down their burger, fries, and soda, and race back to the school gym in time for the music to start. My parents ran a tab for each student, and the parents would come in on Friday to settle up. Mom and Dad had few problems with parents not paying the bill. The moms and dads knew they were getting a bargain, and that their kids were safe during lunch, at least while they were at the shop. Mom always noticed if a student did not show up for lunch, and would call the parents to see if the kid was ill and not at school. Many school skippers were caught because they did not show up for lunch at our shop.

Nearly every student at John Greer Junior High attended the daily sock hops. As students entered the gym, they went to the bleachers, removed their shoes, and donned socks that wouldn't mar the waxed floor. Most students danced; others sat in the bleachers listening to the rock and roll records. The sounds of the Beatles, Rolling Stones, Kinks, and The Monkees filled the gymnasium. Some kids danced well, especially the girls. Most of the boys either rocked from side to side, shuffled around in little circles, or stood in one place while flailing their arms wildly above their heads.

Sock hops were often where new loves were found and lost. Mrs. Mitchell insisted the lights remained on so she could spot any hanky panky going on. Girls peeled sweaters and revealed body parts I never knew they had, and shook in places that were a mystery to me. I was an outgoing fellow, and was not shy about asking girls to dance. I held girls in my arms for fleeting moments and dreamed of things Mrs. Mitchell would frown upon, as Johnny Rivers sang *Poor Side of Town*. Jimmy Ruffin's, *What*

Becomes of the Broken Hearted, became my theme song as I discovered I really – REALLY -- liked girls and wanted to have a steady girlfriend of my very own. I imagined every girl I danced with was "the one." But at the end of the school year, nobody was. I became good friends with many and like a "brother" to all. Nonetheless, Mrs. Mitchell and her Bell Club sock hops had opened up a new side of me that was just starting to emerge and I soon grew confident, and frankly, rather fond of my adolescence.

Mr. Jim Root was my physical education instructor. He was a dynamic man with a haircut so flat, a sheet of paper could sit evenly atop his head. His appearance screamed Marine from top to bottom, but he was calm, and rarely raised his voice. At over six feet tall with his strong, muscular build, his mere presence was intimidating. Mr. Root's P.E. class was always fun and he would play with us as if he was one of us. I couldn't imagine how he found the endurance to play softball, run around the track, or play dodge ball for six hours a day.

In junior high, I was not athletic by any measure. I was still a chunky kid. Mondays were *cardio* days and we had to run 600 yards and do calisthenics. I was usually the last to finish the run and had difficulty with pushups. One kid in my class, George, was the fastest runner and was usually first to complete the set. He constantly needled me about my size. Knowing Mr. Root did not tolerate bullying, I was frustrated that George's comments were always out of earshot of Coach Root. "C'mon, fat boy! Get the lead out! Work off those doughnuts!" I was too proud to cry-baby to Coach Root, and George knew I couldn't fight him if I wanted to. So George kept it up.

One day I couldn't take any more. We were in the locker room getting ready to shower. George again made several comments about my size and my obvious lack of body hair. I waited until he stuck his head under the shower, twisted my wet towel, and snapped it toward his crotch. George dropped like a ton of dung and I left him writhing on the shower floor. Mr. Root quickly stepped in and asked what had happened. I explained, and then took a seat on the bench. Mr. Root questioned George, and to my surprise, his story pretty much confirmed mine.

After we dressed, Mr. Root took us to his office. "Boys, this is going to stop right now. George, do you understand that bullying people does not make them work harder? It just ticks them off. Don, as frustrated as you were, hitting George in the groin was the wrong way to handle it. You two will report to the gym after school." The rest of the day, my emotions were split. I was proud of myself for standing up to a bully; at the same time, I was worried about what Mr. Root had in store for us.

We arrived at the gym just as the detention bell sounded. Mr. Root was waiting at the back door with his stopwatch in his hand. "Get dressed, and come out to the field." George and I dressed in our gym uniforms in separate parts of the locker room. "I'm sorry I flipped you," I said, breaking the silence.

"Yeah? Well, it hurt!" There was a long pause as George pondered some more. "I'm sorry for picking on you," George said while tying his shoes.

When we got to the field next to the school, Coach Root was sitting under a tree twirling his whistle. "George, since you always finish running early and have time to make fun of Don, you will finish as usual, then go back and run with him. Get going!"

Obediently, we took off on our run. Within seconds George was running way ahead of me. I was just trying to put one foot in front of the other without falling. When he finished, George came back and took his place beside me.

"How do you run like that? It seems like it takes no effort," I puffed.

"Running comes easy for me, I guess. We'll work on getting your time down. Don't concentrate so much on your feet and where you're going. Don't think about the end. Get your head up and look around. Get a rhythm in your head, or a song, and try to keep your feet moving to that rhythm. That is what I do." George and I ran together on Mondays for the rest of the year. Mr. Root knew that putting us together and making George help me would help us both. George went on to become a cross country phenom. By the end of junior high, I could not only run 600 yards, but I had lost weight and I was working my way up to running a mile a day.

My shop teacher, Mr. John Green, taught me all the skills I needed to use tools. I had a jumpstart on many guys in this class, though, as Dad had let me help him with the garage remodel on West Penn. I knew how to use a hammer, read a tape measure, cut wood, and had some experience with framing, but I was mostly a task man. Mr. Green, however, taught me to take a building project from conception to completion. I was surprised to learn that shop required a whole bunch of brain cells. We made easy things: a birdhouse, a wood carving, an ashtray. But first we had to design the projects using drafting tools, and then see the projects through. I struggled through Mr. Green's class because I had no patience with detail. Mr. Green made us rework each project until it was perfect. I hated that class, but the skills I learned there are ones I use almost daily in my adult life.

As it turned out, music teachers Jon Dugle, Jim French, and Larry Voorhees had the greatest impact on me during my junior high and high school years. They were regulars at The Do-nut Shoppe. They came in every morning about six-thirty for coffee and doughnuts and discussed their plans for the day's band practice. They laughed easily and always had a joke for Mom and Dad. They always spoke to me and made me feel older.

One day in seventh grade, Mr. Dugle asked me if I had ever played a musical instrument. I laughed and told him not only did I not play, I could not read music. He told me to stop by the band room after school because he and Mr. French wanted to talk to me. I looked at Dad to see if it was all right, and he nodded his approval; Mom, working at the doughnut machine, smiled and nodded her assent. I agreed that I would stop by.

The band room at John Greer was on the second floor of a two story building west of the gymnasium. The bottom floor held the boiler complex for the entire school and the second story was the band room. I was a little nervous when I stepped up onto the second floor because I had never been there and did not know what to expect. The band room was like any other classroom, but once inside, my eyes gazed upon a massive room filled with chairs, instruments, and audio equipment. The floor was tiered so each performer would have a clear view of the instructor, who sat in a chair on a small stage. Giant tubas lined the back row, and that was where I found Mr. Dugle and Mr. French.

"Hello, Mr. Shields, come on back!" Mr. Dugle called. I wound my way through the chairs to the back row, and stood next to him. He blew a loud trumpet on a tuba.

"Nice tuba, Mr. D," I said, as he started what sounded like a musical scale.

"It isn't a tuba, Don," Mr. French interjected, "it is a Sousaphone. It's like a tuba, but it's designed to get the sound up and over the band, so the sound is fuller and not lost up in the air."

Mr. Dugle took his mouth off the mouthpiece, "Wanna try? It is real easy. Just purse your lips and make a flopping sound as you blow through them." He climbed out from inside the instrument, which appeared to wrap itself around the player. I crawled inside and Mr. Dugle presented me with a gold plated mouthpiece. "Here, try this one. That one has my germs on it." He showed me how to replace the mouthpiece and then let me try to play it. The first time I tried, nothing came out but air.

"How do I get sound?"

"Pretend you are giving some one the raspberries, but keep your tongue behind your teeth," Mr. French interjected. "It may take a while to get the hang of it." I tried again, and this time produced a sound that was more like a bodily function than a musical note. We all laughed, and they encouraged me to keep trying. Within about half an hour, I was sustaining a note. I did not know what note, but the sound was a bit more musical. I was hooked! I wanted to continue, but they assured me that the next day my lips would be swollen. I had to work into it slowly. As we talked, these two convinced me that they could teach me to read music and that I could be a functional member of the junior high band, even move to the high school marching band if I progressed well. As they were getting me signed up for band class, Mr. Voorhees appeared.

Larry Voorhees was a small man with an uncanny talent for inspiring students. Like his musical counterparts, he too, wanted to talk to me, but his pitch was about singing in chorus. Me sing? He had to be kidding. I was sure I could not carry a tune in a bushel basket. He invited me to sit at the piano with him and we played a game of *match this note*. Mr. Voorhees would play a short melody and ask me to sing it back to him. I was overjoyed when I found I could do it. And I was good at it! So I joined chorus, too. Within one hour, these incredible, musical men had shown me that I could do things I'd never dreamed of before.

As I left the school, my Mom pulled up in the car and motioned for me to come over. "Don't you have an instrument to bring home?" I knew then I had been set up, but I was thrilled. I was headed toward a world of music and song that would bring me unbelievable joy in the years to come.

CHAPTER FIFTEEN

Our family was much like every other in America. We had a public side and a private side. We argued and bickered at home, but in the shop we put on our happy faces, despite the tensions that sometimes lay just below the surface. Money was tight and we knew we'd never be rich, or have the things other kids took for granted. Jim and I knew our parents loved us, and each other, dearly and it was frustrating for them to be unable to give us all the things we wanted. It wasn't until years later that Jim and I understood and appreciated the sacrifice our parents made when they bought the house on West Penn. They had bought it for us.

Jim and I got on each other's nerves with increasing ferocity. We were both becoming men and our emotions ran high. Both Jim and I wanted to be the alpha male, but in truth, Dad was still the big dog. We constantly butted heads over small things, like mowing the lawn or helping in the shop. Jim was seventeen and looking forward to college and his independence. He had not become rebellious, but pretty much came and went as he pleased. I was still too young to entertain thoughts of leaving home and was jealous of Jim's freedom.

Four years separated me and Jim chronologically, but we were a decade apart when it came to maturity. It seemed he was always upset with me about something. He said I acted like a dufus. One night, as we were in our room while our parents were outside on the lawn enjoying the evening, Jim got mad and threw a baseball across the room at me. It missed, but put a dent in the wall of our shared bedroom. We quickly hung a picture to cover the damage. Another night, Jim came home from working at the American Can and was dog tired. Because of my asthma, apparently I was snoring, sniffling, or just trying to breathe. He took offense to whatever noise I was making and yelled at me to stop. I guess I didn't stop quick enough, because suddenly, Jim was on top of me with scissors to my throat threatening to kill me. He accused me of snickering; I said I was just sleeping! At some point, he relented and got off of me. Fearing for my life, I took my blankets and pillows to the enclosed front porch and spent the rest of the night there. Mom and Dad never questioned why I was sleeping out there, but the unheated porch would be my bedroom until Jim went off to college almost a year later. That winter was not a bitterly cold one, but with the help of an insulated sleeping blanket, long underwear, and a space heater, I survived.

Still, Jim was my brother and I loved him. One night during the Sweet Corn Festival, Jim and his buddies had gone to the carnival across the street, drinking and flirting with girls. Mom and Dad were out for the evening with friends. I heard Jim stumbling about when he came home, and I peeked into our room to be sure he was okay. It was obvious he was severely impaired. When he lay down on his bed, he said it began to spin. He jumped up and opened the window to throw up in the bushes outside, but the storm window was down. He bashed his head into the glass and puked all over the window and the floor. Then he passed out in his bed. The fetid smell of beer, sloe gin, and carney food almost made me retch. While Jim was snoring, I grabbed a bucket and mop and some disinfectant from the shop, and cleaned up his mess. If Mom and Dad ever noticed, they never said a word.

Dad loved to fish in the streams and ponds around Hoopeston. He fished almost every Friday evening and again on Saturday from April until late October. Often he would load up his fishing car, a 1953 Chevy Impala, with plenty of rods and a styrofoam ice chest full of food and beer and would not come home until evening. He enjoyed garnishing a line with a bobber, baiting a hook with a minnow, and throwing it out into the water to let it float. He would sit on the bank of the pond, listen to his transistor radio, and crack open some beers. Dad was mostly a catch and release man, but he did keep his share of crappies, carp, turtles, and frogs. He brought home his catch, cleaned and wrapped them, then put them in the freezer to be served later at a big fish fry for family and friends at the end of summer. Often, after fishing all day, he would pull into the driveway, turn off the motor, and listen to the White Sox game on the radio until he fell asleep. Mom let him be; she knew he would be in when he was ready.

Dad loved baseball, and the White Sox were his team. I asked him why he liked them one time, and he simply explained, "I like where Comiskey Park is located." When I gave him a quizzical look, he responded, "Comiskey is at 35th Avenue and Shields Avenue in Chicago. When they play there, I feel they are family." It was a good enough reason for me. A few times a year, we drove to Chicago to see them play.

I learned an important lesson at one of those games. In 1967, Dad closed The Do-nut Shoppe and took us boys out of school on a Friday afternoon in April. He had never done that before. He announced we were going to Comiskey Park to see the Go-Go White Sox play! The interstate freeway had yet to be built all the way to Chicago, and the Dan Ryan Expressway that now runs by the stadium had just opened. Once we cleared the two lane roads near Kankakee, we had smooth sailing for the two hour trip to the south side of Chicago.

An evening White Sox game in April was a dream come true for us. We were hoping the Sox would hit a homerun so we could watch fireworks shoot from the scoreboard against the night sky.

For youngsters who expect to see a homerun derby at a game, or action on the bases, watching a pitchers' duel is about as exciting as an opera. You get plenty of action, but you don't really understand the intricacies nor appreciate the effort. I was bored through most of the game.

The White Sox were playing the Cleveland Indians that night, and when the Sox went down 3-0 in the top of the seventh inning, I badgered Dad to take us home. I was tired, hungry, and cold. My light jacket was not enough against the chilly April night. We had left Hoopeston around one o'clock, and it was now after eight. Dad and Jim had not wanted to leave, but I was acting like a selfish brat and Dad was sick of my whining. By the time we got out to the parking lot, the game was in the ninth, and Cleveland's lead looked like it would hold up as the Pale Hose had the bottom of their order up. As we reached the car, a roar arose from stadium as the ten thousand fans watched Wayne Causey single to start off the bottom of the ninth for the Sox. My brother shot me a squinty-eyed look as I crawled into the rear seat of our 1965 Ford Galaxy 500. Dad got in behind the wheel and turned on the radio just in time to hear Bob Elson's call of a strikeout by Chicago shortstop Ron Hanson. I felt some of the pressure go off with this first out. Smokey Burgess coaxed a walk out of the Indians' pitcher, Sonny Siebert, who had gone the distance for the Tribe. Ed Stroud, who had replaced Wayne Causey as a pinch runner, stole second, and the tying run came to the plate in the form of right fielder Ken Berry who'd had only one hit that day. He had gotten on base on an error. As we pulled onto the Dan Ryan, Jim shot me another murderous look. I slumped down in the back seat as the Sox loaded the bases for Don Buford. Buford had had a miserable day, and was batting only .163 for the young season, so I thought I was safe. Just then, Bob Elson's voice exploded across the radio with a play-by-play as Buford hit a single into right, scoring Stroud and Al Weiss, who had run for Burgess. Fireworks burst from the scoreboard, which I could only see from the car's rear window.

My dad had missed a chance to see his beloved White Sox win 3-2 against Cleveland, and it was all my fault. I felt ghastly and if there had been food in my belly, it would have certainly come up. Dad didn't say a word during the ride home, but I knew how cheated he must have felt. I learned to never leave a game until the last man is out.

That was the last time Dad was able to take us to a game. We spent many a Saturday afternoon in the living room with him during baseball season, sitting and watching whatever game of the week was on TV. Usually that game involved the Yankees and Pee Wee Reese and Dizzy Dean as the announcers since the CBS television network owned the team. Dad liked baseball because it was rigid in its rules and yet fallible with the human element. Dad often said that baseball was like life. We all have to play the game by the rules and are watched by folks who are supposed to be impartial. If we make a mistake, there are no do-overs, we just have to get right back in there on the next play and try to do the best we can.

CHAPTER SIXTEEN

Jim graduated from high school in June of 1967 and went off to college at Western Illinois University in the fall. I had seldom seen my dad in anything other than his tee shirt and khakis. He actually went out and bought a brown suit to wear to Jim's graduation. He looked dapper in it, and seemed to be a different man. He and Mom were very proud of Jim, as Jim was the first person from our family to graduate from high school and attend college. Neither of my parents graduated from high school. Mom moved around a great deal when she was young and would never be in one place very long. Eighth grade was as far as her education went. Dad was able to attend school until his sophomore year in high school, then he had to quit and help Grandpa Shields in the field mill during the Depression.

With Jim gone, I moved back into the bedroom. Cold winters and hot summers would go by the wayside. Hoopeston housed its freshmen in high school at John Greer Junior High School; so technically, I was in my first year of high school and supposed to be low man in the pecking order, but this year, we were the big dogs in the kennel at the junior high. Sock hops were still our mainstay of social interaction, but no matter how hard I tried to find a girlfriend, I was always the *brother* type and not the *boyfriend* type. I could talk easily with girls, but that was about all. Gholson had a girlfriend and so did Smith, but I seemed to be the subject of that Bobbie Vinton song from 1964, *Mr. Lonely*. My mom said, "Just love them all, Don. You'll find the right one." I had a hard time believing her. I just wanted somebody to call my own, but there were no takers. Maybe I set my sights too high.

This was the year I started to play football. I was not a hard worker, by any means. My sized gave me a certain ability to block, but I was not too keen on throwing myself in front of people who were bigger than I was. Coach Brown put me at center on offense, so I constantly looked at the world upside down and between my legs. The center takes a pounding in the middle from everyone, and I took my share of bumps, bruises, and contusions. I found football was fun and it allowed me to work out some aggression and pent up frustration. We had Derek Baird at quarterback, Fred Sharon at halfback and Butch Drollinger was the fullback. On plays that went straight up the middle over me, if I did not open the hole right away, Butch would surely let me know by plowing straight into me and pushing his way forward like a good fullback should. Don Smith, Dick Rulison, Bill Gholson and Cary St. Clair rounded out the offense. Our defense was pretty formidable too, especially with Butch at middle linebacker. Our freshman team went through a pretty successful season, winning six games. Quite a few of us also played on the junior varsity on Friday nights, so we really played football two nights a week and practiced the other three nights.

But football was not my forte. I enjoyed the contact, the camaraderie, and the discipline, but I was slow and uncommitted to it. There were too many other things going on that I liked better. The band and choral departments had hooked me on their programs, and I was discovering theatre. These activities opened me up. I was able to express myself in song during chorus, and lose myself in acting during theatre. At first, I was just in small classroom plays, but when the spring of 1968 rolled around, I won the lead in the school play: Stephen Lawrence's musical, *Bubble Trouble (or That's the Trouble, Trouble, Trouble with Mr. Bubble, Bubble, Bubblegum).* It was in this ridiculously simple, little musical that I really learned to act and sing. I could not dance a lick (and still can't), but getting up in front of people, making them laugh, and having a good time myself was as rewarding as anything I had done on the athletic field.

With Jim in college and out of my hair, I could relax and just be myself, *Donnie Doughnut.* The Do-nut Shoppe was flourishing and Mom and Dad had started taking special orders from the local businesses for meetings and events. The old doughnut machine was thirty years old and had produced over a million doughnuts. The guys from Food Machinery Corporation and John Deere kept it going by manufacturing parts and making repairs. The shop was still full of kids at lunch time and Mom and Dad loved them all. Aunt Louise, Aunt Harriet, and Aunt Lou all helped out during the day washing dishes and waiting on customers. After school Becky Drollinger would come and help out.

As winter of 1968 faded, the old house on West Penn Street began to show its age. Cracks appeared in the stucco, the front porch was listing forward, and the roof needed to be replaced. Dad took stock of what was to be done and decided the first thing he should tackle was the front porch. The foundation of the porch had begun to crumble, and he crawled under to have a better look. He thought he could jack up the porch, replace the concrete blocks, and let it back down easily. This, he said, was no big task and could be done a little at a time once he had the room up on jacks and blocks. Mom didn't really want him doing it, but she knew better than to discourage him. She knew that if he got into something that he could not handle, he had plenty friends who could help him.

The task of opening the foundation to get to the porch was no easy task. He had to go in through the old coal room, knock out a hole that was big enough to crawl into, and then haul all his tools, jacks, and lights under the porch so he could work. As with all work on old houses, what one finds behind walls is not usually what one expects. He found that the porch was not on a foundation after all, but rather was on posts which were merely set into holes in the ground, much like a deck. He had to change his plans and dig a foundation, then put up blocks to the porch's floor. Dad worked hours on end digging a footing after putting in a full day at The Do-nut Shoppe. There was only about four feet between the ground and the floor, so much of the work was done on his knees with a spade and a bucket to haul the dirt out. I helped him by hauling five gallon buckets of dirt out from under the house and dumping them back by the alley. He worked on this for most of the month of April and made a great deal of headway, getting the footing dug and then poured. On Friday nights, however, Dad usually took a break and went out fishing, or met some friends at the VFW.

May rolled around and Dad was anxious to get the porch finished as good fishing weather was coming around, and the crick bank was calling. He finally got to the point where he could jack up the house and put down blocks. He did not expect the stucco to break as much as it did, cracking from one corner of the porch out to the edge of the house. It was a Wednesday, and Friday looked a long way off, but he needed a break, so Dad decided to go fishing for a while to get his mind off things. Mom told him it was going to rain, but he was insistent that he needed to relax.

As he loaded the '53 Impala with supplies for the evening (ham sandwiches, beer, and bait) he told my mother he would be back early as he was not feeling well. He thought he had a cold coming on, and would probably not stay out much after dark. She reiterated to him that there was a spring storm coming and he could get wet. "I have my rain gear, Al, I'll be fine," he assured her as he left around five o'clock.

When I came home from spring concert practice that evening, Mom said Dad had gone fishing and would be late. We had our dinner and then I tried to do homework. Shakespeare and geometry just did not seem as important as watching the storm roll in or talking on the phone to my friend, Debbie. Debbie and I had become close during our years in junior high. We were like brother and sister (as usual) and we talked constantly. Luckily, she was smarter than I and could help me with geometry. I actually think it was her fault that I flunked that course. She was cute, and I watched her curves and angles more than those in my geometry book. We finished our nightly talk just as the skies let loose with a horrendous downpour. The streets flooded, the wind howled, and trees bent sideways. I thought of Dad out there fishing and I knew he would be soaked. Cold weather and rain made the fish bite better, he always said, so he would sit out there until the lightening and wind forced him to the car. I went to bed early with visions of Romeo and Juliet in my head, knowing that I had to be at school early for band practice.

I awoke the next morning when Mom came into my room and said, "Get up, we have to get Dad to the hospital." Just the mention of the hospital was enough to jolt me out of bed. I hurried into their room and saw Dad lying in bed, propped up on pillows. He had a bluish tint to him and was struggling to catch his breath. "I've already called the ambulance; they will be here in a minute. Go and clear a path for them through the living room," Mom commanded. I took one look at Dad, and did as she said, moving his lounge chair out of the way and the big round coffee table from the middle of the room, and pushed the couch out of the way so the ambulance attendants could get the stretcher in. "Call your Aunt Helen; she is up at Aunt Lottie's house." I had not seen Aunt Helen since Granny's funeral and was not aware that she was in town, but I did as Mom told me.

I called Dad's sister and told her that Dad was sick and we were taking him to Lakeview Hospital in Danville. Hoopeston did not have a hospital at that time, and all emergencies had to go to Danville. She said she would meet us there. I looked out the window and saw the ambulance backing into the driveway.

Hamilton Funeral Home also provided ambulance service back then. There was no 911 service, we dialed "0" and asked for Hamilton's. It was always disconcerting to me that a funeral home would also be the ones to try and keep you alive, but our family had known Gene Orr for years, and he and Dale Brown would do all they could to help Dad. They really did not want to bury people, but help them. They threaded the stretcher across the porch that was under construction, through the living room and into the bedroom. My heart was pounding as I watched them put an oxygen mask on Dad, place him on the stretcher, and cover him with blankets. He did not look good, but I knew he was feisty. Mom leaned over and kissed him goodbye. He looked up at her and said, "Don't forget to put up a sign."

She nodded and whispered, "We'll be there as soon as we can." Dale and Gene wheeled Dad out, carried him down the stairs, and placed him into the back of the ambulance. Then, with a police escort and sirens screaming, the ambulance turned west onto Penn Street, then headed south on Route One to Danville. This would prove to be one of the longest days of my life.

Mom instructed me to put a sign in the window of the shop saying we would be *Closed Due to Illness.* By the time I got the sign in the window, Arnold Schuff was at the door. Schuff was not only one of my parents' best customers and best friends, he was also a police commissioner and had heard the call come in on the scanner. I opened the door for him and he went to Mom, "Tilly, is there anything I can do?"

"Yes, would you make sure the shop is closed and call Lou, Harriet, and Louise? I have to call Jim at school." Schuff assured her he would call the three women, and left to do that. Mom dialed up Jim.

I am sure Jim never expected to get a call from home at six in the morning. "Jim, this is Mom. We are taking Dad to Danville, it looks like he has had a heart attack. No, don't try to come home, I will call you when I know more. We're leaving for the hospital. I love you, too." With that, she hung up the phone, grabbed her keys, and we headed out to the car and to Danville.

I had never seen my Mom so nervous, or more intense in her driving. We turned so fast onto Route One that she squealed the tires on the Galaxy. The big engine in the car roared as we flew down the road. I looked over and saw that her knuckles were white from gripping the wheel. Tears streamed down her face, and she said very little. I could tell her mind was racing. Mom and Dad had been married for twenty-one years, and had been long-time friends before they were married in 1947 in Missouri. Dad wasn't just her husband, he was her best friend.

I'm pretty sure we ran the stop sign in downtown Rossville, and at the intersection of Routes 1 and 136 just north of Danville. As we rounded the curve just before Danville, I remember seeing the old landmarks: the

Indian chief with his bow drawn and the Tin Man with his hand in the air. These two were on the front lawn of a sheet metal shop that, for me, marked the entry into Danville. Every stoplight in Danville was green, and Mom barely braked when we turned the corner at Danville Schlarman High School and sped to Lakeview Hospital.

By the time we parked and entered the hospital, Dad was already in intensive care. Mom was allowed in to see him, but I was made to wait. As I sat in the waiting room, Aunt Helen came out of the elevator and came over to hug me. She did not say much, but asked at the desk if she could see her brother. She would have to wait, also. Dad was only allowed one visitor at a time, and then for just a few minutes. Mom came out and told us Dad was in pain, but they were working to ease that and get him to rest. She told me that I would not be allowed in for a while, and that I should just sit and wait. The day continued to get longer.

I was numb all day. I thought of Jim at Western Illinois University, but I could not call him. His day must have been slow, too. My thoughts drifted in and out about Dad. I didn't want to think about life without him, but those ideas crept into my psyche. What would we do? Who would run the shop? Who would carve the ham? I don't know anything about mixing dough. Then I started thinking selfishly. How will other kids look at me? Will they treat me differently? I had visions of Dad standing behind the fence at Little League, sitting at the counter with his arms folded over his belly, and crawling under that porch to dig it out. I recounted conversations with him, cookouts with him and his friends, family reunions in the park, the last game we saw at Comiskey Park. It all rushed into my mind.

Around one-thirty I was allowed in to see him in ICU. He was a pale white, somewhat pasty with a tinge of blue. I thought that maybe he was this color because of the faint lighting in the room. He wore an oxygen mask and there was a needle in his arm and a monitor that kept a steady beep with his heart. The man that I looked up to, loved, and sometimes feared was not in that bed. He had been replaced with someone frail and semi-conscious. As I stood beside him and stroked his hand, fear grew in the pit of my stomach and made me nauseous. Dad opened his eyes momentarily and glanced my way, but I am not sure he saw me. "Dad, I love you," was all I could say. I stood and stared at him for what seemed like hours, but was only a few minutes. I had no concept of time. I felt as though I was floating, but at the same time my legs felt like iron weights.

The doctor came in and spoke with my mom. "He is stable right now. You should go on home and get some rest. We'll call if there is any change."

We did not want to leave, but the doctor assured us that Dad was okay, and the best thing for us was to go home. Mom relented, made sure that the hospital had our numbers and then led me and Aunt Helen out. She said she would call Jim when we got home.

The ride home was a little more relaxed. Mom talked about how long Dad would be in the hospital, asking the girls to open the shop, getting me back to school on Friday. She had no doubt that Dad would be fine, and we could get Hobie or maybe Kenny Parkinson, who owned the monument shop, to finish the porch. At any rate, it would be a while before Dad would be back at work. She let me know that I would have to take on a heavier load around the house, but assured me that my school activities would not be affected.

As we pulled into the front driveway, I noticed the crack that had caused Dad so much grief. It was a large one, and would have to be chiseled out and then filled in again. As Mom fumbled with her keys to open the front door, the phone rang. She could not find the skeleton key to the old lock. I climbed in the window that opened into the bedroom from the porch, made my way through the disheveled rooms, and opened the door for her. "Hello? Yes, this is Alta Shields. We'll be right there." She turned to me, ashen and near panic. "Dad has taken a turn for the worse. We need to go back to Danville." She dialed up Aunt Helen again, told her the news, and said we would meet her there. She then called Schuff and asked him to get someone to go to Macomb and get Jim. She then dialed Jim and let him know that someone would be coming for him. She tried to stay calm, but the fear crept into her voice. I tried to focus, but the blur had returned to my thoughts as we once again careened down Route One toward Danville.

We zipped past the Indian and the Tin Man with Mom gripping the steering wheel. As soon as we passed them, our right front tire blew. Mom put a death grip on the wheel and steered us to the side of the road. We got out and looked at what used to be a fully inflated tire but was now in shreds. Because of Mom's physical stature, she was unable to change the tire. I had seen it done, but had never actually done it. She put on the emergency flashers and opened the trunk. Just as she opened the lid, my cousin, who was driving Aunt Helen, came to a screeching halt behind us. I told Mom I would stay with the car and she should go on to the hospital.

She said she would call the Danville Police and see if they could come out and get me. They then sped off, leaving me to stay with the car and the flattened tire.

I expected I would have to stay alongside the road for at least an hour. After three hours, I decided to change the tire myself and drive on to the hospital even though I had no official driver's training whatsoever. Car after car sped by me, but no Danville Police, Sheriff's Patrol, or State Police passed by. I tried to remember what Dad had done in the driveway one, and blocked the opposite tire, jacked up the car, and changed the tire. I remembered to check the lug nuts so the tire would not come off. I resolved that I would not drive fast and would stay in the right lane and take my time. Dad and Mom had both let me drive in the country, so I knew basically what to do. Fortunately there was little traffic and I knew how to get to the hospital. I was nervous about trying to drive alone for the first time, but I had to get to Dad.

The sun began to set behind the trees that lined Route One as I took a deep breath, started the car, and reached for the gearshift on the steering column. I checked my rearview mirror and gave a sigh of relief as a county sheriff's car pulled up behind me with its emergency lights flashing. I sat deathly still as the officer strode up next to my rolled down window. "Are you okay, son?" he asked.

"No sir, I ain't." My voice was cracking and I was desperately trying to hold back tears. I went on to tell him about what had happened. He went back to his patrol car and talked into the radio, then returned to my side of the car. "We have been looking for you. Apparently the information that was given to the Danville police said you were in the city limits. When they went to the end of the city limits out here, they did not find a car, so they dropped it. Lock up the car and get in with me. I will take you to the hospital, and we will have someone bring the car there. I did as he said, gave him the keys, and got into the front seat. He spared no expense getting me to Lakeview Hospital, using his lights and siren to speed us through traffic.

When we arrived at the hospital, I thanked him and hurried in the main entrance. Dad was in Intensive Care on the third floor, so I took the elevator just past the main desk. The ride to the third floor seemed to last forever as I anticipated scenarios. The elevator doors opened and my heart began to race as I turned the corner toward ICU. The sun was setting as I saw Mom and Aunt Helen at the end of the corridor, crying. I knew then. "Donnie, Dad's gone," Mom was just barely able to choke out the words as she grabbed me and hugged me. "He had a blood clot that stopped his heart. There was nothing they could do." I broke down and cried as I had never cried before. The pit of my stomach fell to my knees, and I began to feel everything close in on me. When I finally came to my senses, I was standing next to Dad's bed. The nurses had pulled the sheet up close to his chest and he looked as though he was merely asleep. As I stood there looking at him, I marveled at how he looked alive, his chest seemed to move up and down with the rhythm of breathing, but it was just in my wishful mind.

I leaned over and put my hand on his head. It felt cold and hard, with no life in it. He did not appear blue, but was a pale color that could have been from the light above his bed. The dim light shone upwards toward the ceiling, not down on his body. His face was peaceful and smooth, and there was a slight smile on his lips. I imagined he had found the most wonderful fishing hole ever, and was content. Mom squeezed his hand and cried softly, "Jim, what are we going to do? Should I keep the shop open? What do you want me to do? I don't think I can do it alone." Aunt Helen, who was crying into a handkerchief, reached out and put her hand on Mom's shoulder. The two women clutched each other and stood looking at Dad. A nurse came in, and Mom asked her to call Gene Orr at Hamilton Funeral Home to come and get Dad and bring him home. The nurse nodded and left the room. Mom leaned over and kissed Dad one last time, as did Aunt Helen. I was left alone with him. I put my hand on his, said, "See you," and ambled into the hallway, closing the door quietly behind me as if to not wake him.

Mom was on the phone with Jim. I could only hear her side of the conversation, which was very painful to hear. She told him all that had happened and that there was someone on the way to bring him home.

When Jim got home late that evening, we sat up and talked about Dad, about the things he had done, said, and tried. Some of the stories made us laugh. Mom told how Dad had bankrolled the slot machines for the VFW when they were just starting to get the shop going and never told her until he had his money back. Sometimes a person never knows someone until they die, then it is too late. I grieved for the years I would never have getting to know my father.

Jim and I went with Mom to pick out the casket. We picked out something simple that we could afford as we had done for Granny a few years before. Gene Orr informed us that because Dad was a veteran, his headstone would be paid for, and he would get military honors by the

VFW and American Legion at the funeral. We brought up the one brown suit that Dad owned and had worn to Jim's high school graduation just a year before. We all thought it was ironic that Dad almost never wore a suit, just a V-neck tee shirt and khakis, yet we were burying him in a suit so he'd look good. We all thought we should bury a coffee cup with him, but decided not to.

The visitation was long. We saw friends who had been regulars at The Do-nut Shoppe and some whom we'd not seen in years. There were also relatives from Dad's side of the family that Aunt Helen did not even know. Over the next few days, friends, relatives, customers, and even strangers called or sent cards. I was very uncomfortable around people at that time, especially my friends. They did not know what to say, and neither did I. Mostly we just sat together and listened to music or watched TV or went for walks. Debbie, Bill, and Don Smith were especially helpful and did their best to cheer me up.

On Sunday, Jim had to return to school to finish the semester. Before he left, we met as a family to discuss The Do-nut Shoppe. Mom had decided to keep it open, despite some reservations on upkeep. She knew that Aunt Harriet, Lou, and Aunt Louise would help out; her only problem was she had never mixed the dough for the doughnuts. She knew the portions, but the actual mixing was something she had never done, and she did not think she was strong enough to do it.

She and Dad had opened the original Do-nut Shop in July of 1948, and Mom chose July for her re-opening. Since it was already May 16, she would have plenty of time to get up to speed and to be sure things were squared away with Dad's estate. Jim and I said we would help out where ever we could; Jim even offered to quit school. Mom would have none of that, though, as it was Dad's dream to have his boys graduate from college. He had not finished high school, and he wanted his kids to have a solid education. Jim returned to college that evening for the final two weeks before summer break.

On Monday, I got up early to see if there was anything I could do to help Mom. She was already in the shop having coffee while sitting on the stool usually occupied by Dad. She was staring out at the empty shop. Before her on the counter was a to-do list. She had to apply for Veterans Benefits, Social Security for herself, me, and Jim, order a headstone, mow the yard, clean the shop . . . it all was so overwhelming to her.

I was almost fifteen and my life had changed immensely. I, too, had choices to make, but none of them were as pressing as Mom's. I had to just get up the guts to go to school and face the kids. I was worried about how others would view me, a kid without a dad. My first order of business was to get to band practice on time. Band class would help me through my doubts and jitters. Many of the kids in band had been with me over the weekend and I was comfortable with them. I would feel safe there. As I headed for school, Smitty joined me from his house on the hill. He immediately punched me in the arm, and reminded me our regular evening basketball game was on, and then gave me his big, toothy grin. I knew then things were going to be fine.

When Smitty hit me and smiled, I realized that my friends were there for me, and the choices for how I would live my life were mine. My doughnut hole seemed small, but there was plenty of doughy goodness left in my days. People were really not measured by how they live, but rather how they are remembered. Dad would always be either on that crick bank or behind that doughnut machine.

CHAPTER SEVENTEEN

Those first few months after Dad's death seemed shrouded in a mist that never quite cleared. I could remember what he looked like, but I had trouble recalling his voice or things he had said. I wish to this day I could remember the tidbits of wisdom he gave me. Maybe there weren't any, or maybe I never really listened. I wondered if I was ever going to stop missing him. Mom told me that would not happen. He would always be there, and he has been, in the back of my mind. At fourteen, nearly fifteen, I knew there were things I had to do and I did not want to disappoint Mom.

Jim and I began to get along better, but we still fought. Jim came home from college that summer more of a man than when he'd left. He was his own boss after his first year of college. He was able to come and go as he pleased, and I wanted that freedom, too. Quite often when we fought it was because he was giving me advice, and I wanted no part of it. I was a teenager, and I knew it all. I was also at an age where I was not old enough to hold a real job, but too young, I thought, to do menial tasks. Mowing someone's yard was out of the question, although two neighbor guys convinced me to mow their yard.

Sam and Jim had lived across the street from us in an apartment built over their garage. Sam was a teacher at the high school; Jim worked for a canning factory in town. His mother had been a teacher at Lincoln School. They were great guys who played football with us, and were always out doing something in their yard or working on their cars. Dad called them every morning to be sure they were up in time for work, and he had their coffee and doughnuts waiting at the counter when they arrived. Dad made sure they never paid.

Sam had a Corvair convertible he called his "baby," and he worked on it and spruced it up constantly. Not a weekend went by, even in winter, that he did not wash that car, vacuum it, and on warm days, wax it. On winter weekends, he pulled it into the garage below his apartment to work on it. Jim had a truck that he used in his work, and he too, kept his vehicle immaculate. Jim finally bought a house a few blocks away, and he and Sam moved there until Sam married the Spanish teacher he worked with at the high school.

When Jim asked me to mow the yard, I could hardly say no. It would have been like saying no to my older brother. The yard was huge! It took up almost two lots and had a large number of trees on it, and I had a hard time mowing around them. The push mower and the little doughnut boy fought each other all summer. Mom even went out and purchased a mower that was self-propelled, but I still had trouble walking behind it.

The best part of my lawn mowing job is that Jim would leave the door open for me to go inside and cool down on hot summer days. He also left his Playboy magazines on the coffee table. It was through these magazine pictorials and the "articles" that I learned about real women. The "Playboy Advisor" section that was right after the centerfold became my favorite, although I did enjoy the photography a great deal. But the advice offered in the magazine did not seem to apply to girls my age and another summer went by without me having a real girlfriend.

Mom reopened the shop in July of 1968. She did not know what else to do; she had been her own boss for so long. She was also encouraged by customers who would stop by and tell her opening the shop was the right thing to do. So, with help from Aunt Louise, Aunt Harriet, Lou, and Becky, she reopened. She did not do any advertising, keeping with the idea that word would spread. July 14 was chosen because it was Dad's birthday, and he always gave away free coffee on his birthday. This would be no different. And, if people drank coffee, they would buy doughnuts and sandwiches. When The Do-nut Shoppe opened, people were waiting at the door at five AM to get coffee, say hello, and pay their respects. Mom shut down the doughnut machine in the corner during the day only long enough to refill the canister with dough and to give the cutter a quick washing and sharpening. She had wanted to close at two in the afternoon, but there were so many customers she finally got to shut the doors at six. She and the girls were tired, but happy. They would all be back at it early the next morning.

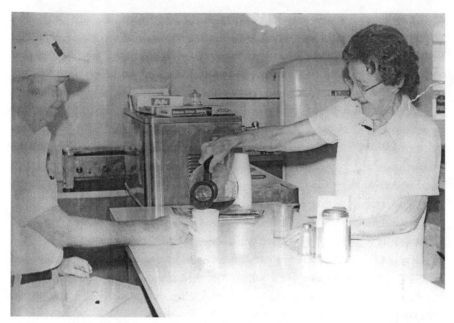

Mom serving Arnold Schuff on the first day of the reopening in July, 1968)
(Courtesty Kankakee Valley Publishing.)

I helped during the day sometimes, washing dishes, waiting tables, and sometimes mixing the dough, but I felt should be doing more. Jim was working at the city and at American Can for the summer and was contributing. I was only an occasional contributor. I did not want to ask for money; I wanted my own, and I wanted to be able to give some to Mom. I had gotten a job at the Little League, taking care of the grounds. I wanted to do more, but I was underage. Finally, with Mom's help, the city hired me to run the concession stand at the Pony League baseball diamond in McFerren Park. The city did not want the headache of running it, so I worked out a deal where the city did not have to pay me, but rather I would run the concessions and take any profit.

That summer I got my first taste of being a boss. I scheduled workers, stocked supplies, and set prices with a fine line for profit. I hired a couple friends and paid them a decent wage of two dollars an hour. Finally, I felt that I was contributing.

The business endeavor was a good one. By the end of summer, I had made enough money to pay for a new stereo for my room, and I had paid Mom for all the extra condiments, doughnuts, food and other necessities I had borrowed for the concession stand. The stereo was an RCA console model with a phonograph and radio built into a cabinet. I was quite proud to have it first in my room, then in the living room of our house. Later, that same piece of furniture would go to my brother's house when he married and moved out. I ran the concession stand one more summer, then the city offered me a job with less risk, that of sewer cleaner and street worker.

Summer flew by with all the different activities I had and the first day of school rolled around. As usual, Mom called Sam to tell him it was time get up. He walked across the street and pulled up a stool next to mine. "Goin' to the Big House today, huh?" He knew very well I was going to the high school.

"Yep, finally going to be a real person, Sam," I answered.

He turned to me and in a very serious voice told me, "When we get to school, it is Mr. Jahn; when we get home, it's Sam, understood?"

I was taken aback by his sudden change in demeanor and I could tell that he meant business. "Yes, sir. Sam?" He chuckled at my questioning tone and turned back to the counter to finish his coffee. I was never tempted to call him by his first name at school.

When school started in the fall of 1968, I went across town to Hoopeston High School and officially became a Cornjerker. Once again, I was a small fish in a large pond, but the pond had changed significantly. There were no class distinctions and no seeming social order. As a sophomore, I was in classes with juniors and seniors. The only one I had with just members of my class was English. That class continued to hold my interest, just as it had in junior high. I took on Latin as an added language. I had taken an introductory class to Latin back at John Greer from Mrs. Jones, so I thought I could handle another class. As much as she tried to talk me out of it, I stayed with her for four years of Latin, a language that is seldom used anymore, even by the Catholic Church. It was there that I learned to conjugate a verb, figure out root words, and roll my R's, a talent which became useful later in life. Mrs. Jones had a tic that she either did not know about, or did not care about. She would constantly lick her lips and seemingly putting her tongue on the roof of her mouth. This became somewhat distracting, and those of us in the class would take sport in betting on how many times in an hour she would do it. I loved that class, and she was an excellent teacher who became a model for me when I began my career behind a desk.

Lots of students find high school constricting. They tend to rebel against all parts of society—their parents, schools, the law, and anything or anyone who might hold them down, or make them adhere to rules.

And in 1968, there was plenty to rebel against. Hoopeston High School had a dress code. The students were tuned in to the changes that were being made in society by the hippie generation, who preached love for all, no restraints on anything, and often took to the streets of major cities to protest "the establishment." Hoopeston kids were a little less vocal, but we still protested, although we took up civil disobedience rather than violence. The boys did not want to wear shirts with collars, belts on our pants, and have hair clipped above our shirt collars. Girls wanted shorter skirts and colored blouses. We wanted the war in Viet Nam to end, and the right to vote and to drink beer at eighteen. Schools all over the United States were loosening up; ours should, too.

About this time, my brother, who was away at college, decided to do his part for the cause, and wrote a letter to the local paper protesting the conflict in Viet Nam. The editor of the paper, Mr. Mills, took umbrage that my brother dared to disagree with his views on the war, and in a resounding letter, tried to put Jim back in his place as a college student who was ignorant of the workings of the world and probably a commie who was trying to undermine the government of this great country. Jim let Mr. Mills know that he was exercising his Freedom of Speech, and Mr. Mills should be a little more open-minded. Mom also let her customers know that she agreed with Jim, and if they did not like it, they could go elsewhere. No one changed doughnut shops.

The article did have a slight backlash for me, though. I was hoping to date a girl who was quite cute, named Susie Dayton, but her father had read the exchange in the paper between my brother and Mr. Mills and decided that if my brother was a "Commie Red" then I surely must be, and no daughter of his was going to date someone who was against this country. Susie, a short blonde with a cute figure, had a great laugh and could sing like a nightingale. When I went to her house to pick her up for a date, her father let me know at the door what he thought, and I never got through the front door. Susie and I remained friends, but dating was out of the question.

The students at Hoopeston High School were able to get the faculty and the administration to acquiesce to some of our demands without any major protests. Boys were soon allowed to wear their shirt tails out, long hair was allowed as long as it was kept clean, no belts, and blue jeans became the order of the day. Girls were allowed to wear miniskirts as long as the top of their hose did not show, and they, too, were allowed to wear jeans and slacks. Suddenly, students began to act like adults. There were fewer fights and shouting matches and students became more involved in the school. In addition to regular classes, the school added flight ground school, graphic design, speech and media courses, and auto shop. The Cornjerkers were on the map for innovation.

My cousins and I became closer than we had been in junior high. Joan was a beautiful brunette with long hair that reached her waist; Rick was a tall, gangly guy who had a great sense of humor and knowledge about cars, which he got from his dad. We all become very close friends, along with Roger Beatty, Don Smith, Bill Gholson, Dennis Reed, John Decker, Ken Kelnhofer, and Randy Garner. We also added a host of upper classmen to our group, including one strange guy, who really intrigued me and challenged me intellectually. His name was John McElhaney.

Unbeknownst to me, John's Mom and Dad, Clyde and Juanita, were regulars at The Do-nut Shoppe, and they were good friends with Mom and had been with Dad. Clyde had worked at the American Can when we were on First Avenue, and was a regular for lunch and coffee breaks. Juanita worked uptown in one of the stores. I guess John and I never really met until we were together in the high school band. John played the clarinet as well as a host of other wind and string instruments. He had a vast amount of trivial knowledge, and was a whiz at chemistry. John, Bill, and I spent a great deal of time together during high school. Mostly we were over at John's house talking about philosophical things, like politics and religion and we listened to John play the piano and organ. He could play anything from ragtime to Bach. It was John who really expanded my love of classical music and even tried to teach me Bach's Toccata and Fugue in D minor on the organ. Unfortunately, my fat doughy fingers could not move fast enough across the keys, and I was too uncoordinated to work the pedals on the organ. But, eventually I was able to play the first part of the Toccata, and saw myself as a virtuoso. John loved pipe organs, and I arranged for him get into the Presbyterian Church where I attended, at any time of the night to practice. When the church burned down, John was devastated. He eventually went to college at Illinois State University and became a chemist, but he never lost his passion for music and photography.

I had many friends and was deeply involved in the social life of the school. High school was a blast by any definition of the word. Band, chorus, and wrestling were my biggest activities. I also dabbled in track and football, but quit both after my sophomore year, and turned my attention to more gentle pursuits.

Band and chorus became my release. I enjoyed performing; it was the practicing that I hated. Jon Dugle, Jim French, and Gary Sauerbrunn did their best to get me to practice my sousaphone, but I just could not get serious about it. They even bought concert tubas, so I learned the fingerings for the tuba relative to their place on the scale, but I never learned to read a bass clef. I tried to play by ear, but could not accomplish that effectively. I never learned to read music and instead would hang back and listen and watch. I was relegated to being second to Randy Garner, a guy half my size who was more passionate about playing the tuba.

Acting was where my talent in the arts seemed to be. It came easily to me, possibly because I didn't mind making a fool of myself. I could pretend to be someone else, and pretty girls loved being on the stage with me. It was amazing looking back on it, how an ugly guy can look so much better when surrounded by pretty girls. The high school musical was a unique animal unto itself. Not only did I have to get on stage and act, but I also had to sing. I drew the line at dancing. For some reason, when I tried to dance, I felt like a cow in rubber boots. I suddenly had feet that would not follow a beat, and wanted to do something that they were totally not supposed to do. I tried imitating Fred Astaire, but I looked like Jerry Lewis on ice skates. My arms went one direction, legs and feet another, and there was no rhythm. All the dancing talent I thought I had in junior high had deserted me; maybe I never had it at all. Acting was a great means of teaching teamwork, though. I never thought that so much went into a play, but when I did "Camelot" as King Arthur, I realized that there were so many parts. I used the planning that went into drama and the creation of characters to get me through my teaching and coaching career after college. I became an actor, and for thirty-four years I played a command performance as a teacher and coach.

The lesson I learned from high school that I used the most came during my wrestling years. I began wrestling in my sophomore year. Coach Jim Richards talked me into going out, because they lacked a heavyweight and I certainly fit the bill. I knew nothing about it, but he said he would teach me. So I decide to try it.

Just at the end of football and before the beginning of wrestling, I had knee surgery. It was nothing major; I had a bone chip in my knee and needed to have it removed. I missed the first two weeks of the season. When I joined the team, we were scheduled to wrestle Danville in a home tournament. I had three days of practice, barely knew anything, and could hardly get my knee bent to get down should I last into the second period.

Coach told me to try and not get pinned, but they needed me to go out and get any kind of points I could. I was to wrestle a guy by the name of Darrell Black, who had taken fifth in state the year before. Darrell was six feet five and weighed about two-eighty; I weighed in at two hundred twenty-five pounds and stood five feet nine inches. The match lasted about fifty seconds and I was able to count ten lights in the ceiling as he drove me into the mat. It was not a very auspicious beginning.

By the end of the year, I was adequate. I got pinned less and won more. The guys on the team gave up calling me *Fish* and called me by my long-time nickname, *Doughnut*. I was able to drop about forty pounds, but I still had to wrestle heavyweight. I hated the practices at first, but by the end of year, all I disliked was the running, everything else had come to suit me.

My second year of wrestling was much better because I came into the season without an injury. I gave up football to march in the band full time, so the greatest injury I could get would be swollen lips, maybe. Knowing more about what was expected of me helped, too. I was able to achieve some success on the mat, even winning a tournament in Indiana.

Coach Richards challenged us both mentally and physically. He ran with us, wrestled with us, and talked with us. In my senior year of wrestling, he came to me and was open and honest with me about my chances for success. I was still a heavyweight, but I was not very strong for a guy my size. I was constantly getting beaten by people who were not as good as I; they were just bigger and stronger. Then a new freshman came on the team. He made me look small. He was athletic and strong. Coach took me aside one evening after practice and laid it on the line. "Doughnut, I know you want to wrestle and you are good technically. But, you cannot compete in your weight class without some muscle. I don't think you can beat Steve."

"Am I off the team, Coach?" I asked him furtively.

"No, we need you, you have a lot of knowledge and you can execute. There aren't many guys your size who can do the moves as well as you. What I want you to do is challenge Steve every week, and help him learn the moves. Make him work in practice so he does not rely on just his size. I will chose when you wrestle in a meet if you don't beat him on challenge night." The team was very good that year, and I did want so much to be a part of it, but I did not know if I could take on such a role. "Take time to think about it; I am asking a great deal from you," Coach said.

My pride was hurt. I immediately thought Coach Richards did not have confidence in me, didn't want me. The team was filled with good wrestlers from top to bottom, and I thought he wanted to fill my space with someone who could win consistently. I had worked hard the past two years, and suddenly I thought I was not appreciated. After talking it over with Mike Dean, a team captain, and Gholson and Smith, who were not on the team, I decided I was not going to go down so easily. I would accept Coach's offer and stay on the team and let him decide my fate if I did not beat Steve.

Getting the best of Steve never happened. He was too big and too strong, and the more we worked, the better he got. He had me, Butch, Dennis Reed, and Dwayne Storm beating up on him in practice every day, and he just kept getting better. During dual meets and tournaments, coaches were allowed to sit next to the mat to coach their wrestlers and Coach Richards would let me sit matside and help coach Steve during tournaments. Finally, one weekend just before the tournament in Indiana that I had won the year before, Coach let me know that I would get to defend my title. By this time, I was down from my beginning weight of 225 to almost 190, but I still had to wrestle at heavyweight, as the cutoff for the next lowest weight class was 185, a weight class already occupied by Butch, our team captain. Butch ranked fourth in Illinois in his class. I was feeling pretty good about getting to wrestle someone other than my buddies and in exhibitions.

As a returning champ, I was allowed a bye in the first round. My first match of the day was against a wrestler from Lafayette who was much bigger than I, but he was slower. I was able to outmaneuver him and get a 7-3 decision on him. My next opponent in the semi-finals was actually my size, and I was able to pin him in the second period. This win set up a championship bout against the same guy I had beaten the year before, John Galliland, from Twin Lakes High School.

John was a good wrestler, and he had gotten stronger since we last met. I, however, was not as bulky as I had been, and I was faster because I had worked every day against Steve. John and I danced around the mat as a large crowd yelled on for each of us. The first period ended with neither of us getting an advantage on the other. I won the toss and started in the down position for the second period. When the referee blew his whistle, I exploded from underneath and escaped to take a 1-0 lead. Takedowns were a near impossibility for both of us and we finished period two with me clinging to my 1-0 lead. John was able to escape from me about the middle of the third period and we once again began to look for an opening for a takedown. The referee thought we were both stalling, so he warned us. That meant if we did not mix it up better, one of us would lose a point for not being aggressive. As we started after the warning, both of us tried for the same move, a double leg takedown. Moving in the same direction at the same time, we collided and I my nose exploded, sending blood everywhere. John was awarded two points for a takedown, and the match was stopped to see about my nose.

Coach rushed in with plenty of cotton and cleaned me up. "Man that looks a little crooked!" he said as he wiped away the blood, "We'd better stop the match."

"No way, Coach! There isn't that much time left and all I need is either a reversal or an escape and a takedown. Let me go!" Richards shook his head, pulled off a big wad of cotton and shoved it up my nose. "Forget the double. Use your speed and either get a single or go for the fireman's carry." He knew I loved both of those, and only the fireman's carry would give me trouble possibly because of the size difference.

I took my place in the middle of the mat on my knees and readied myself for the last half of the period. I took a deep breath and coughed loudly; out came a nasty gob of blood from my throat. The crowd groaned. The referee signaled to get it cleaned up. John and I once again took our positions. As the whistle blew, I came to my feet, slipped out of his grip, and immediately whirled to the single leg take down. John was surprised that I could move that fast, lost his balance as I lifted his leg, and immediately fell awkwardly to the mat. I wasted no time putting him in a half nelson and keeping his shoulders down. The referee pounded the mat, and the crowd exploded with cheers!

I felt pretty good about myself, but I felt even better about Coach Richards. He had faith in my abilities. On Monday, Steve went back to wrestling and winning; I went back to the chair. At the end of the year, Butch made it to state, finishing fifth that year; our team had a good year which started a string of winning seasons in wrestling at Hoopeston.

On recognition night, Coach Richards passed out the awards. Some were statistical, like most take downs, most reversals, or most pins. But the team also gave awards for most improved and most valuable. Steve received the award for most improved. When it came time for MVW, we all knew that Butch would get that. He was, after all, one of the top wrestlers in his class in the state. When Coach Richards made the announcement, he pointed out that the most valuable is not always the most successful. The most valuable is someone who puts the team above self and makes sure that everyone comes together by giving more of himself. He then announced that there were Co-MVWs that year--Butch Drollinger and me.

I could not believe it! All I had done was what Coach wanted me to do. I knew where I stood from the first day of practice and I worked hard to help Steve. I ran every lap to train him, to make sure that he developed. I had only wrestled once all year, and only because Coach let me. It was from Coach Richards that I learned the value of teamwork and that greater things are accomplished when one puts the team before oneself. He was honest with me and knew my abilities, but he never let me get down. He showed me how to use what I had to be successful.

I often view high school as a time when the waters of the river were running. I was blessed just to put my feet in. My grades were average at best, because I did not really have a vision of what I was to become. I had often thought I wanted to be an undertaker, but I think now that was just for effect. I was impressed by the way the morticians handled my family during the deaths of my grandmother and my father, and I saw the nice cars and houses they had. I never really thought it through, however. I believed in an afterlife and by way of logic, ghosts. I knew deep down humans have souls, but what happens right after death? My biggest nightmare would be for a cadaver to rise up as I was doing my job. Would I stab them? Would I scream? Would I load my trousers? I decided that really, I should be something else, but it took me until May of my senior year to apply myself and look into colleges.

Three years had passed since Dad's death. Those were three years of struggling with adolescence and growing up. My friends, my family, my teachers, and coaches helped me through it all. The doughnut machine in the corner kept churning out those globs of gooey delight. The more it kept running, the more my life was enriched, and the icing on those cakes reminded me of the sweetness of life.

CHAPTER EIGHTEEN

The key to getting a girl for a young man, apparently, is a driver's license. Without one, I had to rely on buddies with cars if I wanted to double date, or Mom would drive us to the Lorraine Theatre and then pick us up. The second option definitely lacked cool, and since I was a novice at things like kissing and groping, backseat shenanigans were out of the question while my buddy groped his way through his date in the front seat. Getting my license definitely enhanced my ability to get a girl, but it did not guarantee success.

My sixteenth birthday was in late August just about the time we started the new school year, so I took driver's education in the summer. Coach Richards was also the school's driver education teacher, and I was very comfortable with him. Students usually doubled up to go out with the instructor and one would drive for about half an hour, then the other took his or her turn. Students had to accumulate six hours of behind-the-wheel instruction before they would be eligible to test for their license.

That summer, Coach Richards was taking classes at University of Illinois. One day, when I showed up for my driving lesson, he said, "Doughnut, how about going to Champaign today? I'll let you drive and you can get about two hours in. We'll stop by your Mom's shop and let her know." I was all for it! Smith was also to go with us and drive, too. We stopped by the shop, got the okey-dokey from Mom, and off we went. The drive to Champaign was fifty miles of highway, so there was plenty of time for conversation. We discussed everything from the Cubs to wrestling, and I found out that Coach had previously been a gymnast, and not a wrestler. I was very surprised because he was so very knowledgeable and moved easily on the mat. He told me that he studied wrestling a great deal and went to many matches and coaching clinics to learn as much as he could. One thing about Coach, if he was going to do something, he was not going to go half way with it.

When we arrived in Champaign, he asked me to parallel park the car, something I had never done. But with his direction, I got the hang of it quickly. Once I caught on how to line up my car to get it into the space, the actual occurrence of doing it was easy. Smitty and I got out and started for the building and Coach turned to me. "Where are you going? I have to go to class."

"What are we supposed to do for two hours?" I asked him.

"Papa Del's is over there. Go have some pizza and hang out. It's a college town; find some girls to look at." And with that, he turned us loose. *Well, fine,* I thought. *Our first time on a college campus and we're all alone.*

Coach was right. Midwest colleges, especially University of Illinois, have an abundance of girls, even in the summer. The summer may actually have been better than fall or winter, as these lovely students were lying about on the lawns in shorts and halter tops. To my dismay, none was completely nude, although a couple were lying on their stomachs with straps undone. I found this unsettling and intriguing. With all these pretty girls to look at and an entire deep dish pizza to devour, the two hours passed easily. Coach had to reel us back in and almost pry us from our bench on the Quad at the University of Illinois.

As we headed east Coach decided that we should take Interstate 74 back to Danville so we could experience interstate driving, then north on Route One past the Indian and Tin Man. This time when I passed them, they were smiling and pointing the way home; not exactly how I had remembered them a couple of years earlier the night Dad died. When we got to Hoopeston, Coach asked me to parallel park in front of my house. It was not difficult because there were no other cars at the curb. He opened his door, looked down, and then picked up his clipboard. "Pull back out into traffic." I signaled, checked the lane, and pulled out. "Turn left." I did. "Turn right." I did. "Do a three-point turn." I did. He looked down, scribbled something on the sheet and turned the board over. "Let's go home." As I pulled into the driveway at the shop, he turned the board over, tore off the sheet he had been writing on and handed it to me. "Good job, Doughnut, you passed!" I was overjoyed! My coolness factor had just jumped sky high. He let me out then took Smitty on his way to take his driving exam.

I went into The Do-nut Shoppe and showed Mom. She immediately burst my bubble. "You know, you have to pay for insurance," she stated matter-of-factly. I had never thought about that. How was I going to pay for insurance? "I will float you a loan for your portion, then you can pay me back," she said with that wide grin of hers. "Now, you can really do my running for me!" I wouldn't be pedaling my bike on my errands anymore. I would be driving a car! Suddenly I couldn't wait to do those chores for Mom.

I already had earned my *blue slip* from Coach Richards. Blue Slips were admissions by the state that I had passed my test and all I had to do now was take it to the licensing office and take another test to satisfy the State of Illinois that I really could drive. After taking their written test and a driving test, I was given a temporary license and was told I had to wait for my permanent license to arrive in the mail. I had my first run-in with the law before my permanent license arrived.

Just three days after my sixteenth birthday, Gholson and I took Mom's brand new 1969 Mustang out for an evening of dragging Main. During this rite of passage, we would drive east on Main Street through the downtown area to Market Street, turn south and go one block to Penn Street, then drive west on Penn to Tenth Avenue by my house, turn north one block to Main Street, and then start all over again. It was a monotonous route, but during the drive we would see friends uptown and stop to show off. It was important, I thought, for everyone in town to know I had a driver's license and was allowed to drive my mom's new car. The *cool* kids would pull into a parking lot, usually at Bloyd's Supermarket at the corner of Bank and Penn and start up a conversation with whomever was there. To see and be seen was the whole purpose of the ritual. This was a high school tradition that had been in place for years and years. We would start cruising in the evening around eight, and would be home by eleven, the town curfew on weekdays, and at midnight on weekends.

As we were making our last trip around the horn on this Saturday evening, Gholson dared me to run the stop sign at Fifth Avenue and Penn. Since I seemed to be sitting on my brains at the time, I looked both ways and cruised through the intersection, never seeing the police car parked among the used cars at Burton Motors Sales lot. The cop turned on the cruiser lights and I knew I was busted. I pulled over to the side of Penn Street and waited the eternity it took for the officer to come up alongside me. "Doughnut, did you not see the stop sign?" Orval Kaag, the Chief of Police, had stopped me.

"Yes, Orval, I saw it, but I was in a hurry to get home, and there was no one there or coming; I checked," I said plaintively.

"Well, follow me home. We got to tell your Mom." Suddenly my stomach turned over. I had only had my temporary license for a couple days. I fell in behind him, and he led the way like a little parade with his lights on. He kept them on even when he was in the parking lot of The Do-nut Shoppe. We entered the side door where we found Mom sitting in the dark at the counter. She had been waiting for Gholson and me to come home and had not expected the presence of Chief Kaag.

"Evening, Orval, what did the boy do?"

"Ran the stop sign at Fifth Avenue next to the junior high."

"Don, was it an accident?"

"No, ma'am."

"How much is the ticket, Chief?"

"Twenty-five dollars, Alta. You can give it to me, or come up to the station in the morning. Either way will do." Mom opened the cash register, took the money out of the drawer, and handed it to Chief Kaag.

"How many more does he get before he loses his license?"

"This will go off his record in a year. If he keeps his nose clean, he should be fine. Understand what your Mom just did, young man? She took money out of her pocket to pay your fine. You owe her!" He said goodnight to Mom and walked out to his car. Those lights finally went off. Relief, at last, or so I thought.

Mom gave me that *I'm disappointed* look, the one I vowed I would never get. She turned to Bill and said she would take him home; I was to remain there and we'd talk when she returned.

I waited there in the dark for Mom to return. I think she took the long way around so I would have time to stew about my ticket. She pulled her car into the side drive, parked, and came inside. She glanced at me. That's all. We did not talk. She waited for me to break the silence, but I didn't. After a few seconds, she put the keys down on the counter, and went into the house. I stood there in silence for a minute, and then followed her. "Mom, I am sorry. It won't happen again."

"What won't happen? You won't get a ticket? Or you won't make me stay up worrying about you? I'm sure you will make other mistakes. Just don't make a fatal one, okay? I couldn't stand to lose you or Jim." She turned and went into her bedroom and closed the door.

I vowed I would not get another ticket or make Mom wait up and worry, but my good intentions didn't last long. I was soon to make another mistake, and Gholson would again be along for the ride.

At sixteen, I was crazy for girls, and could not help being distracted while driving through town in the evenings. Even after my promise to be more careful, I still had a few close calls. My friend, Debbie, caused me the most trouble.

Bill and I were out for a drive on an afternoon before school started in August. It was a hot day and we had all the windows rolled down; the Mustang did not have air conditioning. The day had been uneventful and we were headed home, driving down West Washington. As we turned the corner to his house, I spotted Debbie in short shorts bent over a flower bed. I was intent on viewing her at that particular angle and was not at all concerned with my driving. Bill turned to have a look, too, and pulled his arm back into the car just as I cut the corner too tight and hit a power pole, creasing the Mustang from front to rear. Gholson could easily have lost his arm.

When we came to a stop, Bill just looked at me, "What the hell was that?"

"I was a little preoccupied, I guess," I replied sheepishly. The door on his side of the car would not open, so he crawled over the console and got out after I exited the vehicle. Debbie, who lived down the street from Gholson, and her parents were already in the street asking if we were okay.

"What happened, Don?" Debbie's dad questioned.

"I was a distracted and took the corner too close."

"Distracted? By what? The pole is almost in the street!"

"Uh, sir, by something in the flower bed."

He was dumbstruck for a minute, and then he understood. He looked at Debbie, then at me, and broke out in laughter. "Good to see you are okay. We need to call your Mom."

"No, I can drive. I'll go home and tell her. Thanks anyway." Gholson walked to his house, and I limped the crumpled Mustang home. When I entered the house, Mom seemed to know something was wrong. I asked her to come outside with me.

As we walked out the door, she let out a gasp and a, "Oh, Don!" As she examined her car, she simply asked, "Are you okay? Was anyone hurt?" I assured her that the only things hurt were the car and the pole I had scraped. "As long as you are okay," she said. I had gotten a ticket and wrecked her car within two weeks of finishing driver's education, but she still had faith in me. I am certain she was angry, but she held it in very well.

Mom made an appointment to get the car fixed, and we did not report it to the police. I would pay for the repairs myself. I should have known to be more careful. I'd certainly had enough warnings. But before we could take the car to the body shop for repairs, I crunched the driver's side of the Mustang.

When we dragged Main, we would often engage in games of *ditch*, where one driver would try to outrun the other and lose him in a chase. One moonless night just a week after my run in with the pole, I was the chase-ee in a game. I careened down an alley between the Nickel Plate tracks and uptown, turned off my headlights and tried sliding into a space between two buildings. As I did so, I once again cut the turn too short and sideswiped my side of the car, completely creasing the driver's side. The car was still drivable, but it was a mess. Once again, I returned home, told Mom what had happened, and received the same answer, "As long as you are okay." This time, though, when I offered my keys, she did not refuse. She kept my keys until two weeks after all the damage to both sides of the car had been repaired -- a total of one month. I stayed home for the most part, and when I did go out, I depended on someone else to drive. It took me a while to repay my mother for all the damage, but I was never able to repay her understanding and kindness.

News travels fast in small towns like Hoopeston. By the time school started everyone knew about my ticket and two accidents. Getting a date was next to impossible because parents would not let their daughters ride with me. It wasn't until late in marching band season that a girl actually let me take her home from a football game.

Chapter Nineteen

Johanna Road was gorgeous, smart, athletic, shy, and very mature for her age, a year younger than I. I was not in demand among the girls at school, so I was surprised when she sidled up to me, batted those baby brown eyes, and asked if I would take her home. When we got to her house east of town, she invited me in to meet her parents. We all sat together in the living room and Jo's mom offered me cookies and a soda. How could I refuse? Jo's parents were fantastic people and we hit it off immediately. We talked and laughed until around eleven when I called Mom and told her where I was and that I would be late. She gave her blessing and told me to not be too late.

Jo and I talked and laughed until after midnight. She showed me her 4H trophies and ribbons, and I was ever attentive to each word she spoke. As I left, she stopped me at the door, put her arms around my neck and gently touched her lips to mine. I immediately fell in love! No other girl had kissed me like that. I was dizzy, almost giddy, as I drove into town. I knew she was "the one."

Sleeping that night was almost impossible because I kept reliving that kiss, over and over again. I struggled to remember her every word. And that smile. Oh! She had a wonderful smile. I did not feel like her brother. No, not at all. My heart throbbed with anticipation as I imagined holding her in my arms and touching her beautiful face. I wanted to stroke her long, glossy hair, and kiss her again and again. I couldn't wait to see her at school the next day, and ask her out for a real date.

Johanna and I were soon inseparable and I was no longer anxious to spend time with my friends. I wanted only Johanna. We smothered each other with affection and attention. I devoted every ounce of energy I had to making her laugh, making her happy, just to see her smile. That spring we went to prom together and saw the sunrise the next morning. I had never been happier. I even considered not going to college so we could be together all the time. I would just stay in Hoopeston and help Mom run the shop. Mom thought the world of Johanna. I wished Dad could have known her.

It was Mom who noticed that Johanna had stopped coming to the shop as often. But that was okay, I told Mom, because I was spending so much time at her house. When Johanna went away for long weekends with friends, I stayed home and waited for her to return, oblivious to the signs a more experienced man might recognize. Mom suspected all was not well in my relationship with Johanna, but when she mentioned it to me, I blew up and Mom backed down.

After a time, I started to think Mom had been right. Johanna no longer wanted me to pick her up for school, to wait at her locker, or to call her or go out to her house in the evening. I was confused and wondered if I had done something to upset her. We saw very little of each other for a while, and when we did, there seemed to be an elephant in the room. Finally, after weeks of agonizing and dread, I went to her house to talk to her.

I dragged my feet after extricating myself from the car and approached the simple two story frame house with the gray siding. Her dog ran across the barnyard to meet me and wagged his tail excitedly as he jumped on me. He and I were good friends and he often put himself between Johanna and me expecting to be rubbed a little bit. The sidewalk was not that long, but it certainly felt like the final mile that prisoners walk to execution. Johanna's house had been my second home for almost a year; her mom and dad were special to me. As I had so many times, I knocked twice and opened the front door. "Anyone home?" Mr. Road's chair was empty, but Mrs. Road came out of the kitchen with a surprised look on her face, like she was seeing a stranger.

"Don, what are you doing here?" She clearly had not been expecting to see me.

"I was hoping Jo was home. I just wanted to talk to her."

"She's not here. She will be gone for a couple days." Mrs. Road hesitated, and her look turned from surprise to one of misery. "She has not talked to you, has she?" Her mother motioned for me to come sit at the kitchen table. Jo's mom was just like mine, she kept her opinions to herself unless she was asked. She was bothered though, and as she wrung her hands dry, she sat down next to me and extended her hand to lie on mine.

I could feel my throat tightening. "No, what did she need to talk to me about?" I dreaded to think what the answer might be.

"She thinks the world of you, she really does. But her life is taking another direction. She has gone away to be with someone else, someone older. He is in the military. She really should have told you earlier, but she did not want to hurt you." Jo's Mom saw the pain in my eyes, and the anger welling in my neck. "She thinks of you…"

I snatched my hand away and cut her off, "Like a brother." And then my thoughts turned to all the times we had held each other and talked of our tomorrows. Had she seen me as a brother then? I felt physically ill. I stood and gave Mrs. Road a hug, "When she gets home, have her call me. I need to hear it from her. I promise I won't yell." I hoped Mrs. Road saw the strong, self controlled man I wanted her to see. But inside I was falling apart.

For the next two hours, I drove aimlessly, thinking, and wondering – and I sobbed. How could I have been so deceived? My friends had been through breakups before. I don't remember any of them seeming to be crushed with grief. Maybe I was just different than the other boys. One thing I knew for sure was I had to try to convince her to come back to me.

My emotions waffled between anger, self-pity, and indignation. How many others in town knew about Johanna's new boyfriend? Oh, God! Had I been a laughing stock, or maybe someone to be pitied? I felt betrayed and humiliated.

I finally went home and Mom met me at the door. "You look like you've been rode pretty hard there, boy," she said. "Wanna talk about it? She ushered me onto the settee on the front porch and even had an iced tea waiting. Mrs. Road must have called and told Mom what had happened.

"Jo dropped me, Mom. For some guy in the military. How long has this been going on? Did she ever care?" I wanted to blurt out a million other questions, but she wisely closed that door.

"It wasn't meant to be, honey. She was just not the one."

"But how could she be with me all that time and then string me along like a puppy when she was seeing someone else?"

"I doubt if she ever meant for it to go as far as it did," Mom looked straight at me. "She was involved with you, but the real spark was not there. And you were not really in love with her; you were in love with being in love. The sun will rise for another day."

We sat on that porch most of the night and talked about things I never knew. She told me that at sixteen, she had been married to a man much older than she, but he had died. She was young and thought she would never find anyone, but she found Dad. Mom assured me things would work out the way they are supposed to and I would be okay. The sun would rise for another day. If it was meant to be, we would be together again.

Jo finally called Sunday night. "Hey, we need to talk, I guess. Want me to come over?"

"No, I'll come to you. I have a few things that belong to you." I put the receiver back on the hook and picked up the box of things I had already collected. On top was a picture of us together on prom night. I thought I looked dapper in my white dinner jacket and dark pants; she was breathtaking in her long pink gown and elbow length gloves. With her heels on, she was just about my height. I had other mementos, too: a souvenir baseball bat she gave me from a White Sox game we went to, a garter, a ticket stub from our first movie together. None of them mattered much now.

The drive out east of town seemed long, but in a little town like Hoopeston, how long could it possibly have been, really? I took Thompson Avenue and avoided uptown. I didn't want to see or be seen just then. Jo was waiting on the front steps as I pulled in and we met at the driveway. She had been crying and held a handkerchief tightly in her right hand. I crossed in front of the car and met her face to face. "I'm sorry," she started. I wasn't interested in hearing her tell me how she had met a man -- an older man -- and fell in love. I stopped her by putting my arms around her.

"It wasn't meant to be," I repeated what Mom had said. I had other things to say, but I could not choke out the words. "Listen, I hope you're happy. I won't bother you."

I would not drive to her house anymore, or wait at her locker. I knew I would see her at school and I would be cordial, but would not hope for a furtive brush of her hand as I had before. Band trips, with thirty teenagers crowded into a bus on our way to out-of-town football games would be especially hard for me. I wondered if Johanna thought about those things.

I turned, got into the Mustang and drove away. Mom had been right; the sun did come up the next day.

CHAPTER TWENTY

When my senior year started, I was still thinking of Johanna. I missed her terribly, but had let her go to be with the man she chose. I thought there must be something very powerful about the "spark" Mom had spoken of. She had found it with my father. Maybe one day I would find it, too.

I was still confused about what I wanted to be once I left high school. There were too many options for me to grasp, and soon I would have to make a choice. Most of my friends already knew, or at least had an idea, of who they wanted to be and had already started their college search. My future was staring me in the face, yet I was too immature to see myself as a grown man with a college education and a career.

In the fall, marching band was still my favorite activity. We practiced our routines on the football field at seven o'clock in the morning before school started. The crisp air was invigorating most of the time, but as the fall season progressed, it was downright frigid. I could not believe how our baton twirlers braved the cold mornings in their skimpy costumes, which were little more than sequined bathing suits and a pair of short, tasseled boots. They all looked incredible wearing those outfits and sometimes it was difficult to focus on music and marching. Luckily, I marched in the last row with Randy Garner, both of us wrapped in our sousaphones. On several cold mornings, the mouthpiece of my sousaphone would freeze to my lips, and I learned that I had to keep it in my pants or under my armpit to keep it warm when I was not playing.

My good friend, Mel, was an accomplished trumpet player in the Hoopeston High School Marching Band, though Mr. French and Mr. Dugle encouraged him to become our drum major. So, during the summer, Mel attended band camp and learned to be the leader of the band. When he returned from camp, he was not the same person. He displayed a strong, new confidence I had never seen in him before. His voice had deepened to a thunder and projected easily across the field and into the stands. When he strutted along a parade route, his back almost parallel to the ground and his baton pistoning into the air, the crowds *oohed* and *ahhhed*, and applauded loudly. When he barked, "Band! Ten hut!" we wasted no time coming to attention. Mel was our first drum major and he was fantastic. He was also responsible for initiating my next romance.

While at band camp, Mel had met a number of new people, mostly girls, who were studying to become majorettes. A lot of teenage boys would have loved to be in Mel's place, surrounded by beauties, but he was true to his girl back home. He did, however, develop a close friendship with a young lady from Memphis, Tennessee named Debbie.

At one point during the camp, Mel told Debbie of his friend, Don, back in Hoopeston. He assured her I was a very nice guy and well-liked by my teachers and fellow students. He gave her my address and suggested she should write to me. She did, and sent along a picture of herself. She sent not only a wallet sized photo, but also a glossy eight by ten.

Debbie was a vivacious red-head whose looks belied her young age. At seventeen, she was already a charming southern belle. Her first letter to me came in a scented envelope that dripped of the most enchanting perfume. I could almost hear her accent as I read about her. Like me, she was a senior in high school and led the parade as the drum majorette of her band. She loved rock music, and could sing and play the piano. Just from her letters, I thought Debbie sounded perfect. I only saw one problem. She lived in Memphis, about six hours away from Hoopeston. I had heard that long distance relationships were difficult and seldom lasted long, but I was finally ready to put Johanna behind me and take a chance.

Debbie and I talked on the phone almost daily and we really hit it off. We talked about school, marching band, and our families. We even ventured into that now dangerous territory where we wondered what the future might bring for us as a couple. We were anxious to meet face to face.

I talked Mom into letting me take my first out-of-state road trip to Tennessee. Debbie and I burned up the phone lines during the week prior to my visit. The plan was for me to leave Hoopeston after the band's half-time performance on Friday, and drive through the night to Memphis. I would sleep on their sofa, with her parents' permission, of course. When I woke, maybe around noon, Debbie and I would go out to see the sights of Memphis on Saturday, then have dinner with her parents, and go to a movie Saturday night. I would spend the second night again on their sofa. After church on Sunday, I would head for home. It was a good plan, although it left little time for us to be alone. I'm sure Debbie's parents were a bit nervous about leaving their southern daughter alone with a Yankee for too long.

I tried to get Mel or one of my other friends to come along on the trip but everybody was either busy or their parents would not let them go. My driving history was still a subject of some notoriety in Hoopeston.

My late September trip started uneventfully. The drive in the Mustang was comfortable, but I soon found that vast sections of the roads to Memphis were in disrepair. The interstate highways were still under construction and local roads along the interstate route were badly maintained. Most would be torn up after the new highways were completed. Because local roads were closed in places, traffic slowed to a crawl in and around towns and cities, and added hours to my trip. By the time I crossed the Big Muddy into Memphis, I was weary to the bone.

The sun was just peeking over the horizon when I pulled up to the brick ranch home on a cul-de-sac in Memphis. Debbie met me at the front door with a bone crunching hug and a long kiss. When I opened my eyes after our kiss, I saw her father and mother standing in the kitchen peering into the front room. My face flushed with embarrassment as Debbie giggled and introduced us. Her father shook my hand and I was glad to see he was not cleaning a shotgun. Her mother welcomed me with open arms, and like her daughter, gave me hug. Debbie led me to the table where she and her mother had laid out a huge southern breakfast of chicken fried steak, gravy, and eggs. Debbie's father said the blessing and we enjoyed our breakfast and got to know one another.

Debbie's father was a mail man and after breakfast, he set out for work. Her mother made up the sofa with sheets and blankets and I lay down to get some sleep. I was barely able to sleep, however, as I was still rummy from the long drive and excited at meeting Debbie for the first time. What was supposed to be a nice six hour sleep, turned into a three hour nap. I awoke to find Debbie sitting in a chair across from me where she had been watching me sleep. We both smiled at each other and exchanged pleasantries. I showered and dressed, then Debbie and I headed out in the Mustang to see the sights of Memphis.

The day was bright, sunny, and warm in the River City as we made our stops around town. We visited her high school, and drove by Graceland and the hotel where Dr. Martin Luther King had been shot. We ended up in a park not far from her house, where we sat under a tree and talked about everything under the sun. We didn't mention the possibility of having a future together, and I was being oh so careful about not letting myself fall too far, too fast this time. But as the day wore on, I found myself becoming more and more attracted to her. She did have a great smile and always laughed heartily at my dumb jokes.

That evening, after dinner at her parents' house, Debbie suggested we should go watch planes land at the airport. I had never been to a metropolitan airport before and the idea intrigued me. Memphis International Airport was not very big back in 1969, but it did have its share of large planes taking off and landing. We sat inside the terminal and gazed at people as they came and went. We held hands, pecked one another on the cheek, and pretended we were between flights to some exotic location.

The evening ended back at her house where I kissed her deeply before we went inside. No parents this time, just us. I slept very well that night, and dreamed of Debbie.

When we arrived at church the next morning, Debbie introduced me to her friends in the congregation. Everybody was warm and welcoming. *I could move to Memphis after high school,* I thought. *Memphis is a great place and I could see Debbie all the time,* I reasoned. I liked having Debbie sit next to me in church. If there was a sermon that day, I didn't hear it. I was already in heaven!

I left for my drive home from the church parking lot after saying goodbye to everyone. The trip home was uneventful and I arrived safely. At school the next day, Mel was full of questions. All I told him was, "A gentleman never tells." I took a couple more trips to Memphis that fall, before wrestling started. Each time, it was harder and harder to leave Debbie behind in Memphis. I ran up quite a phone bill that winter, as we talked at least three times a week. I did not date anyone else, but I did reconnect with my buddies.

Over spring break that year, I decided to ride my new Honda 450 to Memphis. I couldn't wait to show off my new bike. I left right after school on a Friday and arrived in Memphis about eleven o'clock that evening. This had been my first long ride on a motorcycle and I was beat, but I wanted to see Debbie before checking into the Holiday Inn.

As I turned the motorcycle into Debbie's cul-de-sac, I noticed an unfamiliar truck in her driveway. I coasted into the driveway and removed my helmet and leather jacket. When I strolled up to the porch, I glanced in the window and saw Debbie sitting on the sofa with someone. A guy! I found myself fighting back pangs of jealousy as I rang the bell.

"Don! It's great to see you, come in!" Debbie said not so convincingly with that southern twang. She threw her arms around me and gave me a hug, being careful to not press against me too tightly. It was the kind of hug a girl would give her brother, not her long absent boyfriend.

She led me into the room and the guy on the sofa stood up. He was tall, with short cropped hair, almost military style. "Bob, this is my friend from Illinois, Don. Don, this is my boyfriend, Bob Banyon." Bob must have surely recognized the bewildered look on my face. I had been caught by surprise...again. I decided to keep my mouth shut and see how it played out. I just hoped I had the wherewithal to maintain my cool.

"Nice to meet you, Bob. I was on my way through Memphis on my motorcycle to see a friend in Atlanta, and thought I would stop and say hi." Debbie gave me a cautious glance and put her arm around Bob's waist. She asked if I wanted something to drink and disappeared into the kitchen. "How long you two been seeing each other?" I asked Bob.

"We've been dating since right after New Year. She's a great gal." The proud tone of his voice told me he was stuck on her. When Debbie returned from the kitchen with a pitcher of iced tea and some glasses, Bob and I were exchanging school stories. I shot her a glance and a nod to indicate that I had myself under control and would not cause trouble for her. The stricken look on her face dissolved into one of relief. After Johanna, I resolved that if a girl did not want me around, all she had to do was say so, and I'd go. I just wished Debbie had told me three months earlier. The three of us talked about nothing for a while, and then claiming I was tired from my trip, I excused myself. I told Debbie I would see her the next day and told her where I was staying, as if she didn't know.

The phone rang in my room around ten the next morning. Her voice sounded small and ashamed. "Mind if I come to your room? We need to talk."

"Sure, I'm in 219."

Her knock was gentle and hesitant. I opened the door and motioned for her to enter and she brushed by me quickly. I turned to find Debbie sitting on the bed, her face flush, and her eyes red. I sat down next to her, and she buried her face into the crook of my neck. I, too, grieved as we held each other for the last time. "He's a lucky guy."

"I am so sorry, Don. I didn't mean to lead you on. But we rarely saw each other after Christmas, and it just happened. Can you forgive me?"

"How could I be mad? We were special while we were together. It is tough to carry on when we are so far apart. Whenever I see something about Memphis, I'll think of you." I helped her to her feet, gave her a hug. I brushed back that beautiful red hair from her face, kissed her on the cheek and walked her to the door. "You go be happy." I hoped she did not see the pain in my face. Her car was parked below my room, and she looked up at me one last time as she got in the front seat. Those blue eyes haunted me for a very long while.

I left Memphis late that afternoon. The ride home was exhausting and seemed to go on forever. I crossed into Illinois about eight, just as the sun was setting. Only three more hours to go and I could rest in my bed. The night air and the hum of the bike lulled me into a trance. The Honda 450 began to stutter and I had to switch over to my reserve gas tank just outside Mt. Vernon. The night was extremely dark, and the road took a sudden turn to the left. I didn't, and careened into the tall prairie grass at the edge of the road.

As the motorcycle left the roadway, I felt a sharp pain in my right leg as my body slammed into a metal reflector. I laid the bike down in the ditch, sliding to a stop at the base of a slope quite a distance from the road. My leg was on fire, and could feel it swelling in my pant leg. I was far from the road and far from the nearest town. I passed out from the pain and laid there in the dark.

A road crew found me the next morning as I was coming to from the accident. They were mowing the ditch and had discovered a trail that led to me. They helped me up and asked if I was okay. I assured them I was fine. I told them I had been too tired to ride any longer and I put my bike down and slept for a while. I am sure they noticed I could barely walk. They helped me get the heavy machine up on two wheels. It was drivable. I asked them how far to the nearest gas station. It was just around the curve, about half a mile ahead. I started the engine, straddled the seat, and was able, with great pain, to drive it out of the ditch.

When I arrived at the gas station, I surveyed the damage. The bike was okay, just some grass in the fender and a scratch on the tank. My right leg, however, was black and blue from knee to ankle, and I could barely move or stand on it. I was sure it was broken, but I was far from a hospital. After gassing up the bike, I bought two Sunday newspapers and rolled them up tightly. Then I took off my belt and splinted my leg with the papers. I was able to rest my foot on the pedal, and prayed I would not have to brake hard. The next three hours were torture, and I winced at every bump in the road all the way home.

I arrived home around noon on Sunday. Mom was in her chair outside under the big elm tree as I pulled into the driveway. She immediately noticed my leg. "What happened, honey?"

"I had to put the bike down in a ditch a while back. I may have broken my leg." I didn't tell her that I had spent the night in the ditch, nor did I mention what had happened with Debbie. I was in too much pain, and about to wet my pants.

"We better call Dr. Kosyak. Get into the house and get some ice on it, I'll call Doc." Mom often cooked for Dr. Kosyak's dinner parties, so she had no qualms about calling him on Sunday. He came right over, looked at my leg, and grabbed it hard with both hands, which almost sent me through the ceiling. Then he pronounced it was badly bruised, but not broken. I would have some trouble walking for a few days, but I would be fine.

Doc left and Mom came back into my bedroom. "How you doing?"

"Fine, hurts like crazy, though."

"No, I mean, how are you doing, not how do you feel? Debbie called and told me what happened. She was worried about you. When you didn't call her last night, she got anxious.

"Mom. It's nothing, really. I'm fine. You always told me that if it was meant to be, it would be. But, I really thought this time . . . " Mom gave me a hug.

"You always do, Donnie. You're such a romantic. Give her a call and let her know you're okay."

I hobbled out to the phone and dialed Debbie's number. Her mom answered, "Mrs. B. is Debbie there? This is Don."

"Don, are you all right?"

"Yeah, Mrs. B, I am. I just had a small accident on the way home. Tell Debbie that I will write and tell her about it."

"She's right here. Let me put her on."

That sweet southern voice that I loved came on. "Don, you okay? I was so upset when you didn't call to let me know you made it home. I mean, I didn't really expect you to, but I was hoping you would." Her voice cracked.

"Deb, we're good. I didn't lose my girl; I just got a new best friend. When you look into the night sky and see a plane, think of me." And with that, I replaced the handset. Suddenly the anger welled up inside me and I went to my room and had a good cry. The pain in my leg helped quell my anger, and Mom brought me a chocolate Coke and some doughnuts.

Love, I thought, as I examined my doughnuts, *is like a doughnut. The doughnut is sweet but the hole hurts like hell.* I chuckled at my absurd analogy.

I thought about the two months ahead before my high school graduation. Prom was coming up, and now I had no date. I had planned for Debbie to come up from Memphis for prom and to meet my mother. How silly I had been to believe it would actually happen.

CHAPTER TWENTY ONE

Just days before my senior prom, I still did not have a date. All of my "girl" friends already had dates. I would either go alone or not go at all. I was pretty much resigned to the latter, and had not rented a tuxedo for the occasion. At almost the last minute, and much to my surprise, our foreign exchange student asked me to go to the prom with her. Gabriella Garcia, a Brazilian beauty, had been staying with a local family for the year, while attending Hoopeston High School. It never occurred to me that she didn't have a prom date. If I had known, I would have asked her weeks before. Gabriella had stunning dark eyes and a winning smile. I was delighted to accept her invitation; then I panicked and rushed out to rent a tux.

Hoopeston had only two men's wear stores: Gary's Men's Wear, and Larson's Men and Boys. During prom season, both stores experienced a run on tuxes, and I would be lucky to get one at this late date. Don Smith's mom worked at Larson's, so I went to Martha, who promised to get me a tux. I wanted no ruffles or flourishes, just a tasteful, James Bondsy black tuxedo. True to her word, Mrs. Smith came through and on prom night, I was decked out in a black penguin costume, complete with cummerbund and white gloves.

Walking with this foreign beauty on my arm, I know we looked the part of the handsome couple. I was oh, so debonair, but Gabriella stole the show. She was breathtaking! We strolled into the gymnasium, which had been decorated in an Italian theme. Prom, short for promenade, is a formal ball and a rite of passage into adulthood. We, and all our classmates, certainly looked and behaved as adults of a different caliber and social structure on that special night.

We all danced with our elegant dates to live music. The band, comprised of our music teachers, Mr. Dugle, Mr. French, Mr. Sauerbrunn, and Mr. and Mrs. Voorhees, played songs from the Guy Lombardo genre, and gave the evening a romantic atmosphere. We had a great time until the school administrators pushed us out at eleven o'clock.

After changing out of their formalwear following the prom, most of the kids went to the American Legion. Every year, the American Legion held an exclusive party for the high school seniors and their dates. This party lasted until the wee hours of the morning with loud rock and roll music, games, and prizes. Gabriella and I danced with each other and many of our classmates. By the time the sun rose, we were all exhausted, but the party was still on. From the post prom party, we attended a breakfast at Linda Martin's house out in the country. The Martins were great people who often opened their doors to us. On this morning, they spared no expense in preparing a buffet breakfast. After being out all night, I bid my classmates farewell and went home to bed instead of going with them to Turkey Run. This state park in Indiana was just a short drive from Hoopeston, and many of my classmates went there to camp, hike, and canoe on the Wabash River. I decided to conserve my energy the rest of the weekend to prepare for my final week of high school.

Senior Week, the last week of the school year, was full of special events for graduating seniors. Every day there was something new and fun. We had "Tacky Day," when students were allowed to dress in their tackiest attire. There was also "Senior Teacher Day." I decided to stand-in for Coach Richards and teach driver's education. I wouldn't actually give instruction, so I couldn't hurt anybody. All I had to do was ride around in the back of a car all day.

That morning I dressed in my best khakis, a shirt and tie, and a sport coat, and waited for Coach Richards to pull the driver's education car up to the curb behind the school. Coach Richards sat in the front passenger seat with one student driver behind the wheel; I sat in the back with another student waiting her turn to drive.

I never realized how much Coach took his life into his hands those days on the road. The students were not only unable to drive, many still had trouble starting the car, even at the end of the semester. A sophomore named Terri was to learn parallel parking that day. She did quite well at first, pulling the car next to the vehicle she would park behind, she signaled, and began to back up. She turned the wheel appropriately and the car started to slide into the space. Then Terri either panicked or lost her focus. She might have thought she had her foot on the brake, but it was still on the gas and she gunned it. The car bumped up over the curb in reverse and was on the sidewalk when Coach braked from his side of the car. "A little rough, Terri. Let's pull out and start again. You almost had it. Don't worry this time, okay?" Coach's voice was calm and encouraging. It was like backing over a sidewalk was no big deal. He amazed me at how calm and collected he remained.

Terri pulled her chin off her chest, and with a flushed face and reddened eyes, tried again. This time she slowly, but successfully, backed the car into place. After three more tries, she was a pro. Coach told her to point the carriage toward the barn, and we returned to school to pick up two more driving students. When we were alone, I asked Coach about the lesson. "How do you do it? I mean, aren't you ever scared?"

He smiled at me from the rearview mirror and said, "Sure I am, but I can't let them know it. They would really get upset then!" He went on to tell me stories about near misses with trains, buses, other autos, and deer. He emphasized that, like me, most of his students were now licensed and out on the roads. Then he turned around in his seat to face me. "You know, not one of them has had a wreck or a ticket." He didn't say, "like you have," but I caught his meaning.

By the end of the day, I was so impressed with Coach Richards, I thought I would write in the future plans section of our yearbook, called *Picayune*, that I was "going to college to become a teacher like my hero, Peanut." All the students affectionately referred to Coach Richards as *Peanut* because he was so small. At only five feet-six, most of the boys, and some of the girls towered over him. He was also a very athletic man, and most of the girls had a crush on him. His influence has remained with me to this day and he really was, after my father died, my hero.

On the last day of school, seniors had to attend their regular classes. My Latin teacher, Mrs. Jones, was another teacher who stands out in my memories. She was an older woman who put us through our paces in teaching a nearly obsolete language. Although we never conversed in Latin, she pressed us to learn words, grammar, syntax and how that complicated language was put together. Her class was one of the thorniest learning experiences I ever had, and one that I never mastered. As hard as I worked, I got a "D" in her class.

That last day, Mrs. Jones quizzed each student on their plans for the future. When my turn came around, she leaned forward, took off her glasses, and raised her eyebrows. "Mr. Shields, what do you intend to do with your life?" She seemed to be expecting a sarcastic answer.

"I am pretty sure, I am going to college."

"Where? What institute of higher learning has accepted you?" She had really put me on the spot. I had no idea where I was going!

"I am going where Bill Gholson is going, Eureka College." I thought that might satisfy her, but she kept up the interrogation.

"And what are you going to major in?" My lies were about to trap me, and I started to squirm. Not only had I not applied to any college, I had not even thought about a major.

"English! I want to be an English major and teach school, like you."

I was hoping she would move on to another student. Instead, she put her head in her hands and shook it from side to side muttering, "Oh, what have I done? What have I done?" She stood up, walked to the bookshelf, and pulled out a teacher's edition of an old English Literature text book. She brought it over and laid it upon my desk. "If you are going to mold the minds of America's youth, you are going to need help. Take this and please come back and see me after you graduate from college." She smiled, patted me on the shoulder, and returned to her desk and her inquisition. I opened the book and found all the notes she had written in the margins through the years. I kept that book and used it throughout my teaching career.

Graduation practice that afternoon was somewhat emotional. So many seniors suddenly came to the realization that this very evening, their lives would change forever. Some of the boys would be going to the military and they knew that by June of 1972, they could be in Vietnam. Most of the girls cried because they would be leaving their friends.

Practice went off without a hitch. We were told where to march, where and when to sit, how to accept our diplomas. I didn't know there was so much ceremony and meaning to graduation. Our tassels had to be on the left to begin with, then after all the diplomas had been handed out, we would all switch our tassels to the right to signify that we were now "right" with the world. We would take our diplomas with our left hand and shake with our right over the diploma like we were shaking over a sacred pact of some sort. Everything was done according to tradition. We even had an invocation and benediction by my pastor, Bernie Nord from the Presbyterian Church. All things were as they should be as we vaulted out of the role of juvenile adolescent and into the realm of adulthood.

More than fourteen hundred spectators attended the graduation. Smith and I sat in the front row as we were seated in alphabetical order. I sat and listened intently to our valedictorian's speech; Smith sat and watched her father cry throughout the ceremony. One of those in attendance was my father. I didn't see him, but I knew he was there. He had been there for Jim's graduation in 1967, and I knew he wouldn't miss mine. When I entered the The Do-nut Shoppe that evening for my graduation party, I glanced in the direction of the doughnut machine and I saw my dad, dressed in his white v-necked tee shirt and khaki pants, On his head was his ever-present paper hat, cocked to the right as he always wore it. He looked at me and smiled, nodded his head in approval, and then quietly slipped behind the machine. He had seen his second son graduate and he seemed at peace.

Mom, Aunt Harriet, Aunt Louise, and Aunt Lou spent quite a bit of effort in preparing the feast that was laid out on the counters. There was home-baked ham, burgers, potato salad, cold cuts, and cake. At the very end of the line, in the dessert section, a tray of doughnuts sat conspicuously at the forefront. My days as "Doughnut" were numbered as I began to think about the next step in my life, college.

CHAPTER TWENTY TWO

The Monday following graduation, I scrambled to get into college. After making a stop at the high school to get copies of my transcripts, I drove to Eureka and met with the admissions people, and tried lining up financial aid. To my surprise, my grades were not that bad, but my ACT score of 29 told them I had not even begun to tap into the vast resource inside my head. But even with all the proper paperwork, they said they would have to take my case under advisement because I had applied so late. If I could not get into Eureka College, I was looking at Danville Junior College, which I thought was nothing more than an extension of high school, and that, to me, would serve no good purpose. I told them I understood, and would go home and wait for their decision. The admissions counselor I dealt with, Charlene Policelick, said they would let me know in a couple days. They had to vet all my references and call my guidance counselor to see if I could handle the college work because of my low grades in a few areas like geometry and chemistry. I finished at Hoopeston in the middle of my class and Eureka College wanted students who were above average.

The one hundred mile drive home was long and lonely. I had time to think about all the mistakes I had made scholastically in high school, and vowed that should Eureka give me a chance, I would be a better student. I thought I might attend only a year or two anyway, as I still had the notion of becoming an undertaker.

I returned home and began my summer job working for the City of Hoopeston Street and Alley and Water Department. The two departments had been separate, but with tough financial times, they had merged the two and put them under one manager, Don Miller. Don was a friend of Mom's, a regular in the shop, and I had worked for him for a couple summers doing various labor in the department. The city hired a number of high school boys every summer to do maintenance work for the two departments, so I was around friends and the work environment was fun, but not necessarily challenging intellectually.

Don gave me my own crew that year since I had been through the summer routine before. I was also given charge of a new project: cleaning all the sanitary and storm drain tiles in the city, as well as making sure the sewage treatment plant was kept in working order and looked nice. This job was not difficult, and I had to answer to Gator Garrison, a man of few words, but who loved to tease the boys on the college track. Gator was a former soldier and liked to bark orders, but his bite was not serious, and he knew that sometimes things just did not get done.

My three man crew was myself, Mike Dean, and Mark Samuelson. Dean and I had been in wrestling together, and Samuelson was a trumpet player in band. Since we all knew each other, there was plenty of ammunition for some good natured ribbing. Our job was to clean the sewers from stem to stern starting at the farthest point in northeast Hoopeston and work our way across town pulling the sludge through the sewers to the plant. We were given charge of a new expensive piece of machinery, called a water jet, which was mounted on the back of a truck. Using high pressure, it would blast water through the sewer via a hose with an attached nozzle and clean the tiles as it snaked along. This seemed, at first, to be a monster of a task, but we soon learned that there were some areas that were relatively clean, and we could go through them quickly; other areas needed more attention. Sometimes we would have to call in the guys with backhoes to dig up a tile that had collapsed and replace it. We also discovered that Dean was small enough to fit into manholes better than Mark or I, so he was usually the one elected to inspect the flow through the tiles. Hardly a day went by when we did not end up with human refuse all over ourselves. I spent a small fortune in work clothes, it seemed, and Mom was constantly doing wash. I often went home to shower during my lunch hour. Sewers have a unique smell, a cross between rotten eggs and sundry odors that pounded the senses and there was no getting used to it. That summer was long and hot, and our work was tedious and an affront to our olfactory senses.

We learned volumes about the town through its sewer system by what flowed past on particular days. Weekends and holidays usually meant an increase in sexual activity as the number of condoms flushed down the toilets increased dramatically. During Fourth of July weekend there was an increase in water usage as people had more parties at their homes.

Two weeks after we had begun our odyssey through the town, Gator drove up as we were hosing our way through the northeast section. "Doughnut, your mom needs to see you on break."

"Did she say what she needed?"

"Nope, just called the barn and said you need to check with her on break."

"I'll call her from uptown." We went on break in the morning around nine. We were finished with the northeast part of town so the three of us decided to take the long route and go to the opposite end of town and stop at The Do-nut Shoppe for break instead of going uptown to Larry and Mick's restaurant on Main Street. Many of the guys who worked for the city and the utility companies had coffee at the shop and took their breaks around nine o'clock and there was never a parking space, so we had to park our truck in the alley between our house and Smith's house. Mom always made sure the doughnuts were done by eight-thirty so she could serve the guys and get in on the banter. The machine in the corner sat silent as it normally did about that time of the day as we walked in and took our place at a table under the front window.

Behind the counter on our side of the shop was my Aunt Harriet. She was tall woman who had no trouble speaking her mind and often did so in a gruff manner. Her gruffness was only a cover for a soft heart, and she had to make sure that the guys did not take advantage of her. Whatever they could dish out, she could dish back. "Hey!" she yelled at me as I lumped into a chair at the table. "Get over here and take your buddies their doughnuts and drinks. No one's waiting on you this morning." She had a glimmer in her eye and the corners of her mouth were turned up ever so slightly.

As I walked between the counters to the soda machine, Mom stopped me and handed me a long business envelope addressed to me from Eureka College. It was stamped, *Confidential: Admissions Notice Enclosed.* I took a long breath, grabbed a knife from the silverware tray, slid the serrated edge under the flap, and withdrew the folded letter. Suddenly I didn't want to read it. What if they rejected me? The paper was heavyweight and it felt like cotton. I unfolded the letter. The letterhead at the top revealed the college logo -- a door hewn into two oak trees and surrounded by ivy. I read the first line, "Dear Eureka Red Devil," I was in! I was going to college! The letter also stated that because of my financial status, my ACT scores, and my willingness to participate in the college chorale, I would have to pay only one thousand dollars a year in tuition. I yelled, "I'm in!" and the customers broke into applause. I had never been so relieved in my life!

Mom reached up, put her arms around my neck, and whispered, "I've known for about a week. Miss Policelick called and told me. But she asked me to not say anything until she had all the details worked out. You're supposed to go see her this Saturday."

I called Jim and told him the good news. He was excited for me and reminded me that I had to come up with one thousand dollars. No problem, I told him, my summer job would do the trick.

I was on Cloud Nine the rest of the day and cleaning sewers was never so exciting. On my way home after work, I stopped at Bill Gholson's house. Gholson was gone for the summer in Kentucky staying with his grandparents, but his mom said she would give him the news. I had wanted to room with Gholson at Eureka, but his mom said he already had a roomie. Eureka's campus was small, only a few blocks, so I knew we would see each other often. Mrs. Gholson hugged me and told me that I could be her "eyes and ears." I told her I would, of course, knowing full well I would not violate the unspoken oath of college students, "What happens at school stays at school."

My acceptance into a four year college gave me new confidence. I had trouble in the classroom during high school, but I now put them all behind me to focus on success. That summer I read books that I had should have read in high school: Huckleberry Finn, The Diary of Anne Frank, and Catcher in the Rye. I also thought college inspired sophistication, so I tried to listen to classical music. I had not shunned classical music and the great composers; I had played them in band, but now I listened more intently. Rock and roll was still my mainstay, though, and the pavilion at McFerren Park was rocking with different bands from around Illinois. Every weekend, I went to see the shows: REO Speedwagon and The One Eyed Jacks from Champaign, and Shadows of Night from Chicago. The Jacks were awesome and had cut a few records, but they never made it to the national scene like the other two bands. Their shows were always sold out at McFerren Park.

With my college plans firmed up, I turned to having fun. My motorcycle was never in the garage unless it was raining, and day trips on weekends were the norm. It was not unusual for me and Dennis Reed to take off on a Saturday or Sunday and go across the state, or just cruise for hours, have lunch, then return to home by evening. Neither of us had a girlfriend, and we told ourselves we didn't want girlfriends interfering with our free and easy bike rides. Often, we had company on our motorcycle trips and our rear banana seats carried some very pretty girls. Two weeks before the start of college, Dennis and I were going on an evening ride to Danville to have supper, then return. As we set out, we first rode through town and stopped at Bloyds' Supermarket to see who was hanging out in the parking lot. The lot was packed with kids and cars. Susie Dayton was there with her sister, Louise. Susie was the pretty girl whose father would not let me date her because of my brother's letter to the editor blasting the Vietnam War. Dressed in shorts and a tank top and wearing high heels, Susie approached us as we pulled in among the throng. "Hey, watcha' doin'?" she asked with a slight southern twang that I'd never noticed before.

"Dennis and I are on our way to Danville for dinner; we're taking the back slabs."

"Want some company? Dad is away in Ohio, so I am free."

"Sus, you know your dad would kill us both."

Susie turned to her older sister, Louise, who was sitting on the hood of car nearby, "There's no one around here to tell him, is there?"

Louise sat up straight, gave a chortle, and announced, "No one here is going to spill the beans, sweetie. You know you have to be home by eleven."

I glanced over at Dennis, who rolled his eyes. He knew I would love to have Susie on the back of my bike. "Get on. It'll be fun." Susie was very petite and had to really step up on the footpeg and throw her leg over. She pulled her sunglasses down off the top of her head, wrapped her arms around me, and with a big giggle shouted, "Let's go!" Louise waved and laughed as we rolled to the end of the lot, turned and accelerated east on Penn, Susie squeezing hard as she laughed in my ear.

Dennis took the lead as we wound our way east, then south to Danville. The evening sun was just setting as we pulled into the A&W on the north edge of Danville. Root beer stands were a dying breed of restaurant; McDonald's Restaurants were spreading throughout the country. The days of waitresses on skates rolling with a tray of food to the car were disappearing. This root beer stand and the one in Hoopeston were quickly becoming relics. The look on the waitress's face when she glided up with our order was priceless. Where was she to hang the tray? After some laughter, we told her to put the tray on the picnic table and we'd eat there.

Susie, Dennis, and I sat at that table for over an hour laughing about school, teachers, things friends had done, even Susie's dad not wanting me to date her. My brother and I were the farthest thing from radicals, but her father was convinced we both were bad influences and bound to bring down the country with our political views. Me? I had no political views; I barely read the paper or knew what was going on outside of Vermilion County.

We rode home in the dark with bugs splatting against the fairing of the motorcycle. Dennis headed for his house in Cheneyville as we cleared the Prairie Green slab, and Susie and I rode home alone, she clutched me ever so tightly and pressed against me.

We arrived at Susie's house on East Maple Street around 10:30. She released her hold on me and swung off the bike. She kept one hand on my shoulder as she came around on my left side. "Thanks for the evening. When are you going to school?" She spoke as if she was trying to avoid being heard.

"In a couple weeks. We could do this again, you know." I lifted myself off the bike and turned to face her with my arms around her waist. I never realized how short she was until then.

"Impossible. Dad will be home tomorrow, and then we are moving to Ohio before school starts." Her voice cracked as she gave me this news.

I was stunned. "When did this come about?"

"This week. Dad got transferred to Ohio and our house goes on the market Monday. You're the first one I've told."

All evening I had thought how great it would be if Susie and I could have a relationship, but now she was moving to a new state. I didn't want another long-distance relationship and besides, I was going to college in a few weeks.

"I always wanted to go out with you, you know. One evening…" her voice trailed off as I cupped her lovely face in my hands.

"I'm glad we had this evening. It was fun. Give me your new address and, I will write to you from Eureka." I pulled her close, and we exchanged a sweet, lingering kiss -- our first, and our last.

"I wish I didn't have to go to Ohio," Susie said as she turned to go into her house. I waited until the door shut behind her before I fired up the Honda. I didn't know it was possible to be so thrilled and so sad at the same time. I wondered if disappointment in love would be a recurring theme in my life. "Another love lost," I muttered to myself as I slowly motored down Maple Street toward home.

Gholson came home from Kentucky the next day. I waited as long as I could to go see him, letting his family have him for a few hours. When I could wait no longer, I anxiously walked the three blocks to his house.

There was so much I wanted to tell him about the summer and the coming year. I knocked on the door of the two story frame house across from John Greer and did not wait for an invitation to enter. "Where's little Bill?" I asked of his dad.

"Up in his room. I'll get him." As Bill's dad ascended the stairs, he yelled for his wife and daughters to come out of the kitchen; Doughnut was here to see Bill. Bill's mom came into the dining room with an apron up to her mouth; his three sisters crowded into the doorway. There was something disconcerting, yet deliciously intriguing, about the four Gholson women trying unsuccessfully to hold back their giggles.

Big Bill came down the stairs and told me that Little Bill would be down momentarily, and he went and stood next to his wife. He, too, put his hand over his mouth. I could not even begin to imagine what was so funny. Maybe Little Bill had grown a moustache, or long hair. As he descended the stairs and came into view, there seemed to be no end to his legs. My buddy ducked as he hit the bottom stairs to keep from knocking his head on the ceiling overhang. My God! He was now six feet five inches tall! His shirts did not fit and his pant legs fluttered several inches above his shoes. "Little" Bill had now become "Big" Bill as he towered over his dad and the rest of the family and me. Everyone exploded into laughter as I just stood and stared at my best friend.

"Ghols, what happened?"

"Back hill eatin'," he drawled intentionally. "Momma here used to starve me, apparently. Gramma didn't. Close your mouth, Shields."

I suddenly realized that my mouth was gaping in awe. Bill had grown almost a foot over the summer as his hormones had kicked in. He was a mountain of man, but still that funny guy I hung out with and who would be at college with me. We spent the rest of the day planning our adventures at Eureka College.

CHAPTER TWENTY THREE

The last week before I left for college, Mom was pretty emotional. Jim and his wife, Linda, had moved across the state with their daughter, Sarah, to Milton, Illinois, just east of Pittsfield, where Jim would teach history and coach basketball. Now I would be going away, too. Mom was now sixty, and she still missed Dad desperately. Mom had not lived alone in all her life; she had lived with relatives since the death of her parents. Now she would live alone in her two bedroom house.

I tried to stay as close to home as I could those last few days. We had meals together, watched TV, talked on the front porch or in the shop at night. I asked her why she liked being in the shop alone at night, listening to music. She told me it gave her solace. It was there she felt as if Dad had never left. She said sometimes at night, she would go down to the shop and talk to him out loud.

I came to realize that Mom was one of the most Christian people I knew. A diminutive woman of just over five feet, she had a faith that could not be shaken. She had lived a hard life. Mom had been born in a tent out in the country just before the start of World War I. She had lost her parents and younger sister when she was three to a massive influenza pandemic. She had been shuffled around to live with relative after relative until she was sixteen and went to Chicago to work. Up there she met a man who was older than she, married early, and lost him to a heart attack. She returned to Hoopeston after the outbreak of World War II, married Dad and then lost him to a heart attack. Along the way she had health problems like asthma and open, painful ulcers on her legs. Her faith in God never wavered. She had inner peace.

Mom did not go to church regularly, but she encouraged Jim and me to go as we got older, but never forced us as teenagers. We seldom discussed religion as a family. Mom always told us that if we followed the Golden Rule, our lives would be fine. And she lived by the Golden

Rule everyday. She treated everyone with kindness. I don't remember her ever getting angry with someone in the shop. She always had a gentle way about her, and people were comfortable talking to her about anything and everything.

We began packing things for my move to college. I was in my room filling boxes with clothing and memorabilia. Mom came in, sat down on the bed, and began unpacking the boxes. "Mom, what are you doing? I need those things," I said with irritation in my voice.

She stopped, looked up at me and I saw her eyes were filled with tears. She held my high school letter jacket close to her and blurted, "Why are you leaving me? Don't you know there are things here you should be doing? You should be staying and helping me with the shop. Who is going to mix the dough?" At that moment, with my mom in tears, I felt like the biggest schmuck in the world. She was right, how could I leave her to do all the work? She got up off the bed and left the room. I stood there alone in the middle of my mess having second thoughts about leaving home. After all my travels to Memphis, and around Illinois on my motorcycle; after all the car wrecks and through all the romances and heartbreaks, Mom had stood by me and helped me. Now I was about to start a new life without her.

Mom returned to my room a few minutes later carrying a small box and a cardboard tube. "What's that? I'm not sure I have room for much more," I said, trying not to sound ungrateful.

"Just a couple things I thought you might like," she responded with a smile. "Go ahead, open them. The box first."

She had carefully taped the box and I could not begin to imagine what was inside. As I peeled back the first piece of tape, I immediately recognized the aroma. She had given me a box of doughnuts. "I thought you might need some for the ride." They were my favorite kind, with vanilla icing, and she had frosted them with her own hands. There were more than two dozen doughnuts in the box and all the holes were small.

"Thanks, Mom. I really need these, you know. Maybe I will let them harden and use them as doorknobs." Her smile widened. She knew I was referring to the nickname Dad had given to doughnuts. He called them *doorknobs* because the tasty delights had opened many doors for them.

"Open the tube," she said.

As I began to pry the end off, I could only think of one thing that it could be -- a Farah Fawcett poster, the one where she is wearing a red swimsuit, with her flowing blonde hair and beautiful smile. I had wanted that poster for my room so the guys in the dorm would come in and start a conversation. The poster slid out easily, but it was not Farah. It was the poster of the two jesters from The Do-nut Shoppe. Mom had removed it from its frame and rolled it up for me to take to college. The poster was slightly yellowed with age, but I would be proud to display it in my dorm room. That poster was the best gift Mom could have given me.

We finished packing the car late that night, then sat at the counter in The Do-Nut Shoppe and talked. Mom told me that no matter what I did, she was proud of me. I was about to become the second Shields to go to college and earn a degree. She assured me that I would find the love of my life and I would know she was "the one" because first there would be a spark, then a whole lot of fireworks.

Then she relayed a story I had never heard before. When she and Dad became engaged, they wanted to get married right away, but would have to wait three days for their marriage license. They were so in love, they could not wait. They got into Dad's old Packard, picked up my uncle Don to be their witness, and drove through the night to Joplin, Missouri where there was no waiting period. They were married within hours, and they never looked back or second guessed their decision. I wanted a love like that and I knew I would find it.

When I went to bed that night, the Optimists Creed crept into my dreams:

As you ramble on through life, brother,
Whatever be your goal
Keep Your Eye Upon the Doughnut and Not Upon the Hole.

The next morning, with the jesters beside me on the passenger seat, I was on my way to college. My ramblings had begun.

LaVergne, TN USA
22 July 2010
190382LV00004B/5/P